"YOU GREAT BIG POLICEMAN YOU! YOU COWARDLY SONOFABITCH! YOU LET THEM TAKE MY BABY AWAY! YOU LET THEM!"

Malone just stood there and took it. The rage in his wife's voice. The hate in her eyes. Everything.

The worst part was, he knew this was just openers. The little man named Furia, the big man named Hinch, and the luscious, lethal girl called Goldie weren't finished. They had other things for Malone to do. Things that would turn his stomach . . . sour his soul . . . destroy everything he ever was and ever stood for . . .

And he would have to do them . . .

COP OUT

Other SIGNET Ellery Queen Titles

A novel by
Ellery Queen

COP OUT

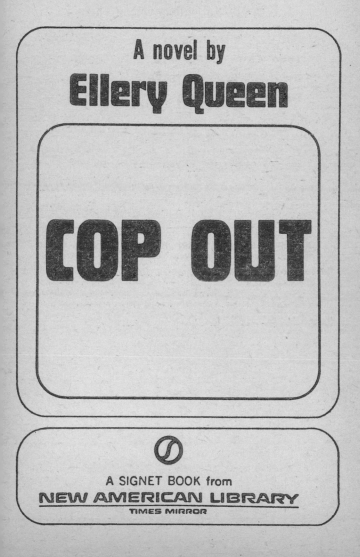

A SIGNET BOOK from
NEW AMERICAN LIBRARY
TIMES MIRROR

Library of Congress Catalog Card Number: 69-12876

This is a reprint of a hardcover edition published by The New
American Library, Inc., in association with The World Pub-
lishing Company, 110 East 59 Street, New York, New York
10022.

SIGNET TRADEMARK REG. U.S. PAT. OFF. AND FOREIGN COUNTRIES
REGISTERED TRADEMARK—MARCA REGISTRADA
HECHO EN CHICAGO, U.S.A.

SIGNET BOOKS are published by
The New American Library, Inc.,
1301 Avenue of the Americas, New York, New York 10019

FIRST PRINTING, MARCH, 1970

PRINTED IN THE UNITED STATES OF AMERICA

We dedicate this
our fortieth anniversary novel
TO OUR READERS,
here and abroad,
who have so loyally followed our adventures in print.

No man is an island, entire of itself.

—*Donne, 1624*

CHAPTERS

Wednesday

The Bag

It had been a good Indian summer and there were still leaves on the tiring maples behind the plant. It was the evergreens that looked expectant, under the moon they stood like girls waiting to be asked by the tall dark handsome sky.

Howland turned away from the window, unadmiring. He hated November. November meant December, and December meant Christmas bills. He had no feeling for nature or religion or almost anything else but money. It seemed to him that for all his fifty-seven years he had been reaching out for money that would stick to his fingers. The irony was that so much of it had passed through them.

He compared his watch with the steel hands over the Manila driftwood door, lettered in computer-type characters CURTIS PICKNEY, *General Manager*.

Almost ten.

Howland went back to his desk. He studied the payroll.

So near and yet so far is the story of my life.

It had started with his first job out of the commercial course at New Bradford High. Old man Louie Wocjzewski had taken him on to tend register in the sandwich shop across the blacktop from Compo Copper and Brass. It had seemed to him then that there could not be so much cash in the world. They were working six-day shifts in those days and eight to nine hundred dollars a week had gone through the register. What he had got from it was twelve greasy singles, counted out in cautious cadence by old Wojy every Saturday night.

It had been worse at The Taugus County National Bank during his cage days when he had handled thousands belonging to everyone in town but Teller Howland. He had not even been able to afford a checking account at first because he had just married Sherrie-Ann and she had stupidly got herself pregnant and sick and then aborted in a mess of hospital and doctor and drug bills, she was still that way throwing their lousy few dollars around like he was a millionaire, my personal dollar drain, Howland's Sewer I ought to call her. Why I didn't ditch her long ago I'll never know, she even makes rotten chowder.

He sat down at his tiny desk before the greenbacks.

He had felt the tiny kick of hope when Curtis Pickney hired him for the new New Bradford branch of Aztec Paper Products. Pickney had spoken rapidly of company expansion, opportunities for advancement (to what?), fringe benefits (and no union), salary to start $103 (take-home $86.75, but you know those g.d. do-gooders in Washington, Mr. Howland), and after nine years he was all the way up to $112.90 take-home and he was still the bookkeeper of the New Bradford branch of Aztec Paper Products. And he would remain its bookkeeper at Pickney's pleasure or until he was hauled out feet first or he made a stink, in which case he'd be still breathing but out on his canister. And where would a man fifty-seven get a decent job in New Bradford? Or anywhere else?

What in hell is keeping them?

As he thought it he heard the triple knock at the back door of the plant.

Howland jumped.

One, two-three.

But he stood there.

The payroll was in undistributed sheafs of rubberband-ed bills beside the canvas bag as he had brought it from the bank in the afternoon accompanied in their every-Wednesday waltz by Officer Wesley Malone, the town cop

11

with the eyes that always seemed to be scouting for Indian sign or something.

I wonder what Wes would think of this, probably stalk me like he did the bobcat that showed up from Canada or someplace and played hob at Hurley's chicken farm. And put a bullet between its eyes.

The thought turned about and it strengthened him. Still, as Howland hurried to the back door through the dark plant his lungs labored and his heart punched away at his Adam's apple.

But his head held trueblue to his plans. They did not include Sherrie-Ann. They did not even include Marie Griggs, the twitch-britches night countergirl at Elwood's Diner.

He was not sure what they did include.

Except $6,000.

A year's pay practically, tax-free.

Howland unlocked the door.

Hinch was at the wheel. My wheelman, Furia called him. Hinch drove into the empty parking lot behind the plant and stopped the car on the tarmacadam ten feet from the rear entrance. It was a Chrysler New Yorker with a powerful purr, like Hinch. Black satin under the dust and not a dent. Furia had picked it out personally on the main drag in Newton Center, Mass. in broad daylight. They had switched plates on a back road near Lexington and Hinch crowed. It was a sweet bus, the neatest they had ever copped. It even had a police band on the radio. Furia was sitting up front with Hinch. Goldie was in the back seat flipping one of her Lady Vere de Vere cigarets, goldtipped what else.

Furia got out.

He had a stiff's skin, tight and yellow, and Mickey Mouse ears. Goldie, who was gone on *Star Trek* and Leonard Nimoy, had once called him Mr. Spock for a gag, but only once. Furia wore an executive three-button Brooks, a no-iron white shirt, a bleak gray silk tie, a two-inch Knox, black gloves, built-up heels, and amber goggles, the latest type, that made him look like a frogman. His London Fog he had left on the front seat.

He stood there like a spinning top, motionless to the eye. He looked around.

"No." He had a spinning sort of voice, too, so hard and tight it practically sang.

12

Goldie stopped in the act of stepping out of the car. Hinch did not move.

"Why not?" she asked.

"Because I'm giving you the word."

"Bitch," Hinch chortled.

Furia looked at him. Hinch gave him a rather embarrassed spread of the hand.

"I gave you the word, Goldie."

Goldie shrugged and stepped back into the Chrysler banging the door. When Goldie shrugged her long gold hair shrugged with her. She had borrowed the effect from the TV commercials. She was all gold and scarlet, a girl of bottles and pastes. Her miniskirt came eight inches under her crotch. She was wearing gold fishnets and tall gilt boots.

Her eyes sat on purple cushions, not eye shadow.

"Looks okay," Hinch said.

"Don't kill the engine just in case."

"Don't worry, Fure."

Furia stepped up to the plant door. He walked on the balls of his feet like an actor playing a thief. As he walked he felt for his shoulder holster the way other men feel for their zippers.

He knocked three times. One, two-three.

The pair in the car sat very still. Hinch was looking into the rearview mirror. Goldie was looking into Furia.

"He's taking his sonofabitch time," Furia said.

"He chickened out maybe," Hinch said.

Goldie said nothing.

The lock turned over and Howland stood in the moonlight like a ghost in shirtsleeves.

"Took your sonofabitch time," Furia said. "Where's the gelt?"

"The what?"

"The moo. The payroll."

"Oh." Howland yawned suddenly. "On my desk. Make it snappy." His teeth clicked like telegraph keys. He kept sneaking looks at the deserted lot.

Furia nodded at the Chrysler and Hinch got out in one move: he was behind the wheel, he was on the macadam. Goldie stirred but when Furia gave her the look she sat back.

"Has he got the rope?" Howland asked.

"Come on." Furia jabbed at Howland's groin playfully.

The bookkeeper backed off and Hinch laughed. "What's the stall? Let's see that bread."

Howland led the way, hurrying. His steps echoed, Furia's and Hinch's did not. Hinch was wearing gloves now, too. He was carrying a black flight bag.

Howland's desk was in a corner of the outer office near the window. There was a greenshade light over the desk.

"Here it is." He yawned again. "What am I yawning for?" he said. "Where is the rope?"

Hinch pushed him aside. "Hey, man," he said. "That's a mess of bread."

"Twenty-four thousand. You don't have to count it. It's all there."

"Sure," Furia said. "We trust you. Start packing, Hinch."

Hinch opened the flight bag and began stuffing the bundles of bills in. Howland watched nervously. Into his nervousness crept alarm.

"Hey, you're taking too much," Howland protested. "We had a deal. Where's mine?"

"Here," Furia said, and shot him three times, one-and-two-three in a syncopated series. The third bullet went into Howland no more than two inches above the first two as the bookkeeper's knees collapsed. The light over the desk bounced off his bald spot. His nose made a pulpy noise when it hit the vinyl floor.

Furia blew on his gun the way the bad guy did it in Westerns. It was a Walther PPK, eight-shot, which he had picked up in a pawnshop heist in Jersey City. It had a double-action hammer and Furia was wild about it. "It's better than a woman," he had said to Goldie. "It's better than you." He picked up the three ejected cases with his left hand and dropped them into his pocket. The automatic he kept in his right.

"You cooled him pretty," Hinch said, looking down at Howland. Blood was beginning to worm out on the vinyl from under the bookkeeper. "Well, let's go, Fure." He had all the money in the bag, even the rolls of coins, and the bag zipped.

"I say when we go," Furia said. He was looking around as if they had all the time in the world. "Okay, that's it."

He walked out. Hinch lingered. All of a sudden he was reluctant to leave Howland.

"Where's the rope, he says." When Hinch grinned his mouth showed a hole where two front teeth had been. He

14

was wearing a black leather windbreaker, black chinos, and blue Keds. He had rusty hair which he wore long at the neck and a nose that had been broken during his wrestling days. His eyes were small and of a light, almost nonexistent, pink-gray. "We forgot the gag, too, pidge," he said to Howland.

"Hinch."

"Okay, Fure, okay," Hinch said. He catfooted after Furia, looking pleased.

"I knew it," Goldie said. Hinch was backing the Chrysler around.

"You knew what?" Furia had the flight bag on his lap like a child.

"The shots. You killed him."

"So I killed him."

"Stupid."

Furia turned half around and his left hand swished across her face.

"I don't dig a broad with lip neither," Hinch said approvingly. He drove across the lot on the bias, without lights. When he got to the turnout he braked. "Where to, Fure?"

"Over the bridge to the cloverleaf."

Hinch swung left and switched on the riding lights. There was no traffic on the outlying road. He drove at a humble thirty.

"You asked for it," Furia said.

There was a trickle of blood at the corner of Goldie's pug nose. She was dabbing at it with a Kleenex.

"The thing is I don't take names from nobody," Furia said. "You got to watch the mouth with me, Goldie. You ought to know that by this time."

Hinch nodded happily.

"What did you have to shoot him for?" Goldie said. In his own way Furia had apologized, they both understood that if Hinch did not. "I didn't set this up for a killing, Fure. Why go for the big one?"

"Who's to know?" Furia argued. "Howland sure as hell didn't sound about our deal. Hinch and me wore gloves and I'll ditch the heater soon as we grab off another one. So they'll never hook those three slugs onto us, Goldie. I even picked up the cases. You got nothing to worry about."

"It's still the big one."

"You button your trap, bitch," Hinch said.

"You button yours," Furia said in a flash. "This is between me and Goldie. And don't call her no more names, Hinch, hear?"

Hinch drove.

"Why I plugged him," Furia said. "And you had a year college, Goldie." He sounded like a kindly teacher. "A three-way split is better than four, I make it, and I never even graduated public school. That shlep just bought us an extra six grand."

Goldie said fretfully, "You sure he's dead?"

Furia laughed. They were rattling over the bridge spanning the Tonekeneke River that led out of town; beyond lay the cloverleaf interchange and the through road Goldie called The Pike, with its string of dark gas stations. The only light came from an allnight diner with a big neon sign at the other side of the cloverleaf. The neon sign said ELWOOD'S DINER. It smeared the aluminum siding a dimestore violet.

"Stop in there, Hinch, I'm hungry."

"Fure," Goldie said. "My folks still live here. Suppose somebody spots me?"

"How many years you cut out of this jerk burg? Six?"

"Seven. But—"

"And you used to have like dark brown hair, right? And go around like one of them Girl Scouts? Relax, Goldie. Nobody's going to make you. I'm starved."

Goldie licked the scarlet lip under the smudge on her nostril. Furia was always starved after a job. At such times it was as if he had been weaned hungry and had never made up for it. Even Hinch looked doubtful.

"I told you, Hinch, didn't I? Pull in."

Hinch skirted the concrete island and drove off the cloverleaf. Neither he nor Goldie said anything more. Goldie's face screwed smaller. She had a funny feeling about the caper. Fure was flying. It never works out the way I plan it. He always queers it some way, he's a natural-born loser.

Hinch swung the Chrysler into a slot. A dozen others were occupied by cars and trucks. He turned off the ignition and started to get out.

"Hold it." Furia turned to examine Goldie in the violet haze. "You got blood on your nose. Wipe it off."

"I thought I wiped it off."

16

He ripped the tissue from the box over the dash, spat on it, and handed it to her. "The left side."

She examined her nose in her compact mirror, scrubbed the smudge off, used the puff.

"Do I look all right for Local Yokel?"

Furia laughed again. That's twice in three minutes. He's real turned on. He'll try to be a man-mountain in bed tonight.

"We don't sit together," Furia said to Hinch. "You park at the counter. Goldie and me we'll find a booth or somewheres."

"That's using your tank, Fure."

"Goldie don't think so. Do you, Goldie?"

He was sounding amused. Goldie risked it. "Does it matter what I think?"

"Not a goddam bit," Furia said cheerfully. He got out with the black bag and made for the diner steps without looking back.

That's what I love about you, you're such a little gentleman.

The diner was busy, not crowded. Furia went in first and snagged a booth from four teenagers who had been nursing cheeseburgers and malts. Goldie managed to join him at the cost of a few stares. She saw no one she recognized. She slipped behind the partition and hid her miniskirt under the fake marble top. I told Fure I ought to wear slacks tonight but no he's got to show off my legs like we're on the town, these studs will remember me.

She was angrier with Furia than when he had struck her.

Hinch slouched in a minute later and settled his bulk on a stool a few feet away. He became immediately enchanted with one of the girls behind the counter, who had just come out of the kitchen. The girl had sprayshine black hair done up in exaggerated bouffant and a rear end that jerked from side to side as she moved.

"You'd better watch the pig," Goldie said. "He's already got his piggy eyes on a girl."

"Don't worry about Hinch," Furia said. "What'll it be, doll? Steak and fries? Live it up."

"I'm not hungry. Just coffee."

Furia shrugged. He had stripped off his gloves and he began to drum on the table with his neat little nails. His

Mediterranean eyes were glazed. In the glare of the fluorescents his skin had a greenish shine.

The diner was jumping with soul music, orders, dishes, talk. There was a lively smell of frying onions and meat. Furia drank it in. The overcast in his eyes was from pride at his achievement and regret that these squares could not know his power. Goldie had seen it before, a recklessness that would later rush to relieve itself. She had her own needs, which involved perpetual thought. His violence kept her squirming.

"Hey, you," Furia said. The girl with the versatile rump was delivering a trayful of grinders to the next booth. "We ain't got all year."

Goldie shut her eyes. When she opened them the girl was clearing the dirty dishes from their table. She was leaning far over, her left breast over Furia's hands.

"I'll be right back, folks." She flicked a rag over the table and seesawed away.

"That chick is stacked what I mean," Furia said. "As good as you, Goldie."

"I think she recognized me," Goldie said.

"You think. You're always thinking."

"I'm not sure. She could have. She was starting high school when I left New Bradford. Her name is Griggs, Marie Griggs. Let's split, Fure."

"You make me throw up. And she did? It's a free country, ain't it? Two people having a bite?"

"Why take chances?"

"Who's taking chances?"

"You are. With that bag between your legs. And packing the gun."

"We'll take off when I've ate my steak." His lips were thinning down. "Now knock it off, she's coming back. Steak medium-well, side order fries, two black. And don't take all night."

The waitress wrote it down. "You're not having anything but coffee, Miss?"

"I just told you, didn't I?" Furia said with a stare.

She left fast. His stare warmed as he watched her behind. "No wonder Hinch got his tongue hanging out. I could go for a piece of that myself."

Flying all right.

"Fure—"

"She didn't know you from her old lady's mustache."

18

His tone said that the subject was closed. Goldie shut her eyes again.

When his steak came it was too rare. Another time he would have turned nasty and fired it back. As it was he ate it, grousing. Steaks were a problem with him. Cooks always thought the waitress had heard wrong. He hated bloody meat. I ain't no goddam dog, he would say.

He hacked off massive chunks, including the fat, and bolted them. The fork never left his fist. Goldie sipped carefully. Her skin was one big itch. Psycho-something, a doctor had told her. He had sounded like some shrink and she had never gone back. It had been worse recently.

Hinch was working away on the girl behind the counter, and she was beginning to look sore.

One of these days I'm going to ditch these creeps.

At eleven o'clock, as Furia was stabbing his last slice of potato, the shortorder man turned on the radio. Goldie, on her feet, sat down again.

"Now what?"

"That's the station of Tonekeneke Falls, WRUD, with the late news."

"So?"

"Fure, I have this feeling."

"You and your feels," Furia said. "You're goosier than an old broad tonight. Let's hit it."

"Will it hurt to listen a minute?"

He sat back comfortably and began to pick his teeth with the edge of a matchpacket cover. "First you can't wait to blow the dump—"

He stopped. The announcer was saying: "—this bulletin. Thomas F. Howland, bookkeeper of the Aztec Paper Products company branch in New Bradford, was found in his office a few minutes ago shot to death. Mr. Howland was alone at the plant, preparing the payroll for tomorrow, when he was apparently surprised by robbers, who killed him and escaped with over twenty-four thousand dollars in cash, according to Curtis Pickney, the general manager, who found the slain bookkeeper's body. Mr. Pickney was driving by on his way home from a late Zoning Board meeting, saw lights in the plant, and investigated. He notified the New Bradford police and Chief John Secco has taken charge of the case. The Resident State Trooper in New Bradford is also on the scene. A search is being organized for Edward Taylor, the night security guard, who has disappeared. Police fear that

Taylor may also have been the victim of foul play. We will bring you further bulletins as they come in. In Washington today the President announced . . ."

"No," Furia said. "Stay put." He nodded at Hinch, who had turned their way. Hinch was blinking his pink eyes. At Furia's signal he tossed a bill on the counter and ran out with two truckdrivers who had jumped up and left their hamburgers uneaten.

"I told you, Fure!"

"Say, Miss America, how's about two more coffees?"

The waitress took their empty cups. "I can't believe it," she said. "That nice old guy."

"Who?"

"That Tom Howland."

"The one they say got shot? You knew him?"

"He ate in here all the time. Used to bend my ear by the hour. I can't believe it."

"You never know," Furia said, shaking his head. "Step on those coffees, huh, doll?"

She went away.

"Some day you'll learn to listen to me," Goldie muttered. "I told you to just tie him up. No, you've got to go and shoot him."

"Goddam it, Goldie, you bug the living hell out of me sometimes, you know that?"

They drank their second cups in silence. There was no music in the diner now. The cook had turned the radio off, too. People were arguing about the robbery and murder. Furia said, "Now," and rose. Goldie slid from the booth and made her way safely to the door. Furia, carrying the black bag, strolled up to the counter and said to the waitress, "How much for the lousy steak and javas?"

Goldie slipped out.

Hinch had the motor running when Furia got in beside him. "Turn on the police band."

Hinch turned it on. The air was full of directives and acknowledgments. The state police were setting up roadblocks throughout the area.

"Now what?" Goldie had her arms folded over her breasts. "Big shot?"

"You want I should shove your teeth down your throat, is that what you want?" Furia said. "I ought to let Hinch work you over."

"Any time, pal," Hinch said.

"Who asked you? I got to think."

"What's to think?" Hinch said. "We hole up in the hideout till the heat goes away, like we said. No sweat. Let's drag, Fure."

"If you had a brain you'd be a dope." Furia had a roadmap of the area spread on his lap under the maplight. "To get there from here we got to cross this intersection. There's no other road in. That'll be one of their main checkpoints. We can't make it tonight. We got to think of something else."

"You'd better get rid of the gun," Goldie said remotely. She was burrowed as far as she could get into the corner of the rear seat.

"Not till I get me another one."

"You going to kill somebody else for one?"

"I told you!"

"Why didn't you take the watchman's gun?"

"Because it landed in some bushes when we jumped him. We couldn't hang around looking for it in the dark. I'll get one, don't worry."

"It's a wonder you didn't shoot him, too."

"You're asking for a rap in that big moosh of yours, Goldie. I'm telling you! When Howland sent this Taylor into town for coffee and we hit him on the road, he put up a fight and we had to cool him with a knock across the ear. We tied him up and threw him in some bushes. How many times I got to tell you?"

Hinch said, "We parking here all night?"

"Let me think!"

Goldie let him think. When she thought the time was ripe she said, "Maybe if we think out loud."

Furia immediately said, "So?"

"The watchman can't finger you, you hit him in the dark. Nobody saw us at the plant except Howland, and he's dead."

"That's why I hit him. That and the extra cut. But you got to make out like I'm a dumdum."

"If we'd worked it the way I said," Goldie said, "he'd have cut his throat before he fingered us. But I'm not going to argue with you, Fure. The big thing went sour was the manager driving past the plant. So now we're hung up here. For a while they're going to stop every car trying to leave New Bradford."

"I know," Hinch said brightly. "We bury it."

"And have the paper rot or be chewed up? Or somebody find it?" Goldie said.

21

"We sure as a bitch ain't throwing it away," Hinch growled.

"Who said anything about throwing it away? It's got to be put somewhere safe till they stop searching cars. The shack would be good, but we're cut off from there till they get fed up and figure we made it out before they set up the blocks. Meantime—the way I see it, Fure—we need help."

"The way she sees it," Hinch said. "Who's fixing this match, Fure, you or her?"

But Furia said, "What help, Goldie?"

"Somebody to keep it for us."

"That's a great idea that is," Furia said. "Who you going to ask, the fuzz?"

Goldie said, "Yes."

Hinch jiggled his bowling-ball head. "I tell you, Fure, this broad is bad news. Some joke."

"No joke," Goldie said. "I mean it."

"She means it," Hinch said with disgust.

Furia picked a sliver of steak out of his teeth. "With a farout idea like that there's got to be something in it. What's on your mind, Goldie?"

"Look," Goldie said. "I've been keeping in touch with my family off and on through my kid sister Nanette—"

"That is absolutely out," Furia said. "I ain't stashing no twenty-four grand with a bunch of rubes."

"Are you kidding? They'd break a leg running to Chief Secco with it. Ma's the big wheel in her church, and my old man thinks having a bottle of beer in your car is a federal offense." Goldie laughed. "But Nanette's no square. She's looking to cut out one of these days, too. I know from her letters. She does a lot of baby-sitting nights and one of her steady jobs is for a couple named Malone, they have a kid Barbara. The Malones live in a one-family house on Old Bradford Road. It's one of the original streets of the town, never any traffic, and the neighbors pull their sidewalks in at nine o'clock. Well, Wesley Malone is a cop."

"There she goes again," Hinch said.

"On the New Bradford police force."

"What gives with this dame?" Hinch demanded of Taugus County. "Some idea! We should park our loot with the town cop!"

But Furia was heavily in thought. "How old did you say their kid is, Goldie?"

22

"Must be eight or nine by now."

"You got yourself a deal."

"But Fure," Hinch protested.

"That's the beauty part," Furia said. "A cop's got to know the facts of life, don't he? He ain't going to panic and try something stupid. Okay, Hinch, get going."

"Where to?" Hinch asked sullenly.

"This Old Bradford Road. Direct him, Goldie."

Goldie directed him. They went back into the cloverleaf and across the bridge, past three blocks of midtown, and sharply right into a steep road called Lovers Hill, Goldie said, because there was a parking strip on top where the town kids necked. Halfway up she said, "Next right turn," and Hinch turned in grudgingly. There were no street lights, and towering trees. It was a narrow street, almost a lane, lined with very old two-story frame houses in need of paint.

The road swooped and wound in an S. At the uppermost curve of the S Goldie said, "I think that's it. Yes. The one with the porch lit up."

It was the only house on the street that showed a light.

"Almost," Furia said, sucking his teeth, "like they got the welcome mat out."

Ellen began praising the film the moment the house lights went up.

"Not that I approve of all that violence," Ellen said as her husband held her cloth coat for her. "But you have to admit, Loney, it's a marvelous picture. Didn't you think so?"

"You asking me?" Malone said.

"Certainly I'm asking you."

"It's a fraud," Malone said.

"I suppose now you're a movie critic."

"You asked me, didn't you?"

"Hello, Wes," a man said. They were being nudged up the aisle by the crowd. "Good picture, I thought."

"Yeah, Lew," Malone said. "Very good."

"*Why* is it a fraud?" Ellen asked in a whisper.

"Because it is. It makes them out a couple of heroes. Like they were Dillinger or somebody. In fact, they used some stuff that actually happened to Dillinger. You felt sorry for them, didn't you?"

"I suppose. What's wrong with that?"

"Everything. Nobody felt sorry for those punks at the time it happened. Even the hoods were down on them. The truth is they were a couple of smalltime murderers who never gave their victims a chance. Clyde got his kicks out of killing. His favorite target was somebody's back. Hi, Arthur."

"Great picture, Wes!" Arthur said.

"Just great," Malone said.

"It got the nomination for Best Picture," Ellen sniffed. "You're such an expert."

"No expert. I just happened to read an article about them, that's all. Why kid the public?"

"Well, I don't care, I liked it," Ellen said. But she squeezed his arm.

The Malones came out of the New Bradford Theater and made for their car. Ellen walked slowly; she knew how tired he was. And how stubborn. Loney had insisted on following their Wednesday night ritual, which involved dinner at the Old Bradford Inn in midtown and the movies afterward, even though he had not slept eight hours in the past ninety-six. It was the only recreation she got, Loney had said, flattening out his chin, and she wasn't going to lose out just because the flu hit the department and he had to work double shift four days running. He could get a night's sleep tonight, Mert Peck was out of bed and Harry Rawlson was back on duty, too.

"How about a bite at Elwood's?" he said at the car. It was a beatup Saab he had picked up for $650 the year before, their old Plymouth had collapsed at 137,000 miles. The big Pontiac special he drove on duty belonged to the town.

"I don't think so," Ellen said. "I'm kind of worried about Bibby. Nanette had to leave at ten thirty, her mother's down sick, and I said it would be all right. But with Bibby home alone—"

"Sure." He was relieved, she knew every pore in his body. Then she saw him stiffen and turned to see why.

One of the New Bradford police cars had torn past the intersection of Grange Street and Main along the Green, siren howling. It was being chased by several civilian cars.

"I wonder what's up," Malone said. "Something's up."

"Let it. You're coming home with me, Loney. Get in, I'll drive."

Malone got in, and Ellen went round and took the wheel. He was looking back at Main Street and she saw

24

him feel for the gun under his jacket. Ellen hated Chief Secco's rule about his men carrying their revolvers off duty.

"Lay off the artillery, bud," Ellen said grimly, starting the Saab. "You're going nowhere but beddy-bye."

"It's something big," Malone said. "Look, Ellen, drop me off at the stationhouse."

"Not a chance."

"I'll only be a couple minutes. I want to find out what gives."

"I'll drop you off and I won't see you till God knows when."

"Ellen, I promise. Drop me off and go on home to Bibby. I'll walk it up the Hill."

"You'll never make it, you're dead on your feet."

"That's what I like about you," he said, smiling. "You've got such confidence in me."

Grange Street was one-way below Main and the Green, and Ellen sighed and turned into Freight Street and past the dark brown unappetizing railroad station. She had to stop for the light at the corner near the R.R. crossing. Malone was squinting to their right, across the bridge and the Tonekeneke and the cloverleaf to The Pike. Two state police cruisers were balling south on The Pike, sirens all out. Ellen deliberately jumped the light and turned left.

She made another left turn east of the Green, drove the one block up to Grange again, and swung right. The Colonial redbrick town hall stood at the southeast corner of the Green and Grange Street, extending into Grange; the New Bradford Police Department was near the rear of the building, with a separate entrance. The entrance was a little windbreak vestibule. There were two green globes outside.

Ellen stopped the car. He was on the sidewalk before she could put on her emergency.

"Remember, Loney, you promised. I'll be hopping mad if you doublecross me."

"I'll be right home."

He hurried inside and Ellen peeled off, taking her worry out on the Saab.

To Malone's surprise no one was in the station but Sam Buchard, the night desk man, and Chief Secco and a middle-aged woman. The chief was over in the corner at the steel desk normally used by the Resident State Trooper, and he was talking to the woman seated beside the desk. Her makeup was smeared and her eyes looked worse than Malone's. She was smoking a cigaret rapidly. Buchard was making an entry in the case log. The LETS—the Law Enforcement Teletype System out of the state capital—was clacking away as usual in its cubicle behind the desk.

Malone walked around the glassed partition to the working area. Chief Secco looked up with a disapproving glance and went back to his interrogation. The woman did not turn around. The desk man said, "What are you doing here, Wes?"

"Sam, what's up?"

"Didn't you hear?"

"I was at the movies with Ellen."

"Murder and robbery over at Aztec."

"Murder?" The last homicide in New Bradford had been four years ago when two men and a woman from downstate had decided to try some illegal night fishing off the railroad trestle over the Tonekeneke. They had been tanked up and the men had got into a fight over the woman. One of the men had fallen off the trestle into thirty feet of water and drowned. Malone and Mert Peck and Trooper Miller had fished his body out the next morning fifty yards downstream. Malone could not recall a bona-fide Murder One in all his years on the New Bradford force. "Who was murdered, Sam?"

"Howland, the bookkeeper. Shot three times in the chest. The payroll was stolen."

Malone recognized her now. Sherrie-Ann Howland, the one the women called "the bloodsucker." She had never even given Tom Howland the excuse of being unfaithful to him. Townspeople rarely saw her, she was said to be a secret drinker. She was sober enough now. Malone knew nearly everyone in town, its population was only 16,000.

"Any leads, Sam?"

"Not a one. The state boys have set up roadblocks throughout the area. Curtis Pickney found him by a fluke, and they say Howland wasn't dead long. So maybe the killers didn't have a chance to get away. Anyway, that's the theory we're working on."

Malone knuckled his eyes. "Where was Ed Taylor?"

"We just found him."

"For God's sake, did Ed get it, too?"

"No, they slugged him, tied him up, and threw him in some bushes. Ed says there were two of them. No I.D., it

26

was too dark. They took Ed to the hospital. He'll be all right. He's a lucky guy, Wes. They could have shot him, too."

Malone hung around. Secco was still questioning Mrs. Howland. He took the log and pretended to read it. The familiar form—B. & E. and Larceny, One-Car Accident, Etc., Obscene or Harassing Telephone Calls, Non-support, Driving under Influence, Stolen and Recovered Motor Vehicles, Resisting Arrest, Destruction of Private Property, Attempted Suicide—had ghosts in it like the TV sometimes. He dropped the log and wandered over to the cabinets. Each officer had a drawer for his personal property. He opened his and fingered its contents—summons book, warning book, his copy of the motor vehicle laws, tape measure, a torn-off brass button Ellen had replaced and then found in the lining of his leather duty-jacket, a crayon self-portrait Barbara signed BIBBY TO MY LOVING FATHER in multicolor curlicue capitals, a copy of a five-year-old income tax return. He shut his drawer and took a Hershey bar from the department commissary drawer, depositing a dime in the cashbox. He stripped off the paper, dropped it into the waste basket, and chewed the chocolate slowly. Chief Secco was still talking to the widow.

Ellen will have my hide . . .

Malone took inventory. The E & J Emergikit on the counter—resuscitator, inhalator, aspirator. The two-watt, two-channel walkie-talkie. The case with the camera and flashbulbs. Nothing changes. Only for Sherrie-Ann Howland. I hope he left some insurance. It's a dead cinch Pickney didn't pay him enough to sock anything away. The whole town knew Pickney's and Aztec's way with a buck. And there was all that talk about Howland and Marie Briggs at Elwood's. How do you kill in cold blood? A man had a right to live out his life, even a life as sorry as Tom Howland's. A woman had a right to a husband, even a woman like Sherrie-Ann.

Secco rose. Mrs. Howland got up in a different way. As if her back ached. "You sure you don't want me to have one of the boys run you home, Mrs. Howland?"

"I parked my car in the town hall lot." There was nothing in the widow's voice.

"I could have it delivered to you in the morning."

"No." She walked out, past Sam Buchard, past Malone,

27

past the partition, through the vestibule. She walked stooped over like a soldier holding his guts in.

"Goddam," Sam Buchard said.

"Oh, Wes," Chief Secco said. "One thing. When you met Howland at the bank today and took him back to the plant with the payroll, how did he seem to you?"

Malone was puzzled. "I didn't notice specially."

"Did he act nervous?"

"Well, I don't know. He talked his head off."

"About what?"

"A lot of nothing. Now that I think of it, maybe he was nervous. Why?"

"All right, Wes," Chief Secco said. "Out."

"Chief," Malone began.

"Didn't you hear me?"

"John, you'll need all the help you can get."

"When you went off duty, Wes, what did I tell you?"

"You said take a couple days off—"

"Then do it. We're under control here. I'm not about to have you come down with exhaustion. I've told you— more than once—this isn't a one-man department. Believe it or not, I've got ten other men most as good as you."

"Four of them trainees."

"That's my problem. You leaving under your own steam, Wes, or do I have to run you out?" Secco looked as if he could do it. He was almost sixty but he had a steer's build and a tough face under the gray crewcut. He was home-grown New Bradford like most of the force. His father had been a dairy farmer and he had grown up tossing hay bales and stripping teats. He still had a knee-buckling grip.

"All right, John, but just one thing. How does it look to you?"

"An outside job, I make it. I didn't tell Mrs. Howland, but I think Howland was in on it and got crossed. That's why I asked you if he seemed nervous this afternoon. Now get out, will you?"

"You can't leave me hanging, John! What's the indication of that?"

"Ed Taylor says Howland all of a sudden sent him into town for coffee. Ed thought nothing of it at the time, but after he got slugged and came to it struck him funny. Howland never did that before. Looks to me like a setup: Howland got Ed out of the way so he could let the robbers into the plant. He'd probably dickered for a cut

28

of the loot, and after making the deal they shot him down. Go home."

"Any hard evidence?"

"Not yet."

"Mrs. Howland have any ideas?"

"She can't see two inches past her own miseries. Go home."

"Who's at the plant?"

"Trooper Miller. He's waiting for the state lab men and the coroner. Go home, Wes!"

Malone left on dragging feet, not all from fatigue.

He walked east to the corner, turned right, did the one block past the Ford agency to Three Corners, and started up Lovers Hill.

How did a man get to the point of kicking his whole life away? Even a life as rotten as Howland's? Or maybe that was the answer. Howland's wife was a drag and a drain, his job was a lot of nothing, he was going nowhere, he was in his upper fifties, and he handled a lot of other people's money. It made some sort of cockeyed sense if you were in Howland's shoes. He had never seen a happy look on Howland's face, even at the times when he dropped into Elwood's for a coffee on a cold night and caught the guy playing up to Marie Briggs.

He wondered if the Briggs girl was involved. No, Marie was too smart. Besides, she had a thing going with Jimmy Wyckoff and it looked serious. Jimmy was a good-looking kid who pulled down a good salary as a machinist at Compo Copper and Brass. If there was anything between Marie and Howland it had all been in Howland's head.

Malone felt a rush of affection for his own girls.

Suppose I didn't have them? Suppose Ellen had turned out a nag and a spender like Sherrie-Ann? And as lousy in bed as she must be? Suppose Ellen had miscarried with Bibby, as she had done twice before and once since Bibby was born, when Dr. Levitt advised her not to get pregnant any more? There would be no little girl with copper curls and a valentine for a face and those big honey eyes full of love for the hero in her life. (And hadn't Ellen been floored when, at the age of six, Bibby had climbed into his lap and clutched him around the neck and looked deep into his eyes and asked, "Daddy, do you love mommy more than you love me?" He could still see the expression on Ellen's face.)

Malone turned up into Old Bradford Road.

No, life would be as big a zero as Howland's without his girls. Until he had met Ellen, with her snapping Irish eyes and tongue, he had never been serious about a girl. He had never had a girl. Only girls, and most of those had been the kind who drifted in and out of Rosie's over on Lower Freight, and they didn't count. He had never had any close friends of either sex before Ellen. It was Ellen, with her insight into people, who had quickly seen him for what he was and dubbed him The Malone Ranger, from which he became "Loney" to her and to her alone.

He found himself smiling as he trudged around the curves of the S. In bed sometimes he called her Tonto, just to get her mad. ("If you haven't found out the difference between Tonto and me yet, Wesley Malone, you need a course in sex education!")

He had always had to make out. His father, a cold and silent man, had worked on the roads for the state, and Malone's memories of him were colored by the black oil he could never seem to clean off his hands and face. He had died when Malone was thirteen, a stranger, leaving a bed-fond widow who chainsmoked and never combed her hair, and four younger children. They were girls, and he became the man of the house before he had to shave. It still made him mad when he thought of the monthly check from the town welfare fund. It provided just enough to keep them from starving, and an inexhaustible supply of ammunition for the town kids. He had hunted up work for after school, swearing to himself that the first time he could make enough to turn down the town handout he would kick somebody's teeth in. He did his studying at night—his mother insisted, with a stubbornness he now recognized as the source of his own, that he go through high school. During the summers he mowed lawns, bagged groceries at the supermarket, farmed out for the haying season, painted divider lines on the roads. Anything to earn a dollar. He turned it all over to his mother. Money meant little to him except as it kept her from complaining.

By the time she died of lung cancer in New Bradford Hospital, his sister Kathleen was old enough to cope with the household and the younger girls. He began bringing his earnings to Kathleen. He had supported his sisters through high school, he had seen them safely married, he had kissed them goodbye as one by one they left town with their husbands and kids, wondering whether he would ever

30

see them again. Most of them he never had seen again, although he got a letter once in a blue moon, usually griping, they came by their complaining ways honestly. And his favorite, Kathleen, was living in San Diego on the base, her husband was career Navy, and he did not hear from her at all.

He had never played Little League ball, he had never joined 4-H or a club at high school, he had never prowled the town with a gang on Halloween, he had never gone dragging on The Pike with other teenagers when the car bug hit. Instead, when he had been able to slip off into the woods with his .22, a hand-me-down from his father which he had kept fiercely cleaned and oiled, he pretended to be a Marine—wriggling through the brush on his belly, drawing a bead on the snapping turtles that infested Balsam Lake (and never shooting except at the empty gin and whisky bottles with which the Lake woods abounded)— always by himself. Somewhere along the road he had lost or strangled the need for group enjoyment. By the time he was free and on his own, the boys he had grown up with avoided him and the girls laughed at him as a square. That was when he had spent so much time at Rosie's.

One of his recurring regrets was that he had been too young for Korea and too old for Vietnam. He had enlisted in the Marines instead of waiting to be drafted and spent two of his four years on sea duty in the Med, all drill and mock-landings and spit-and-polish and the whorehouses of Barcelona, Marseilles, Kavala, Istanbul; the rest of his hitch he sulked at Parris Island handing out fatigues and skivvies to frightened recruits. He was not, his C.O. told him, a good Marine, too much rugged individualism and not enough esprit de corps. He was a lance corporal twice and a corporal once; he wound up a Pfc. His only achievement of record was the Expert Medal he earned on the firing range. He formed no lasting friendships in the Corps, either.

It was John Secco who had talked him into joining the New Bradford force. He had always looked up to Chief Secco as a fair man, his standard of goodness. Secco had an understanding of boys. His policies had kept the juvenile delinquency rate in New Bradford among the lowest in the state.

"I won't kid you, Wes," Secco had said. "You'll never get fat being a town cop. You'll have to learn how to handle selectmen, sorehead taxpayers, bitching storekeep-

31

ers, Saturday night drunks, husband-and-wife fights, kids out to raise Cain, and all the rest. A good smalltown policeman has to be a politician, a squareshooter, a hard-nose, and a father confessor rolled into one. It's almost as tough as being a good bartender. And all for a starting pay of eighty-some bucks. I've had my eye on you for a long time, Wes. You're just the kind of man I want in my department. There's only one thing that bothers me."

"What's that?"

"Can you follow orders? Can you work with others? Can you discipline yourself? Your Marine record says you can't."

And he had said, "I don't know, Chief. I've done some growing up. I think so."

"All right, let's give it a try. Take your training at the state police school, and let's see how you make out on your six months' probation."

He had chalked up the best record of any recruit in the New Bradford department's history. But he thought that John Secco still had questions in his eye. John and Ellen. They sure hold a tight rein on me. And it's not so bad.

The porch light was on, which meant that Ellen was waiting up for him. Leave it to Irish. The Saab was in the driveway, too, not put away. She had probably left it handy in case he failed to show in what she considered a reasonable time and she decided to drive back down into town to haul him home by the ear.

As he turned into his gate Malone paused. There was a strange car across the street, a black dusty late-model Chrysler New Yorker sedan. No one on Old Bradford Road could afford a car like that. It was parked at the Tyrell house, but the house was dark, so the people couldn't be visiting. The Tyrells rarely had visitors, and never so late at night, they were an old couple who went to bed with their chickens. The people from the Chrysler might have been visiting the young Cunninghams next door, but the Cunningham house showed no lights, either. Maybe I ought to check it out. But then he remembered Ellen's look at the stationhouse and decided that discretion was the better part of whatever it was.

Malone trudged up the walk and onto his porch, reaching for his keys. He felt suddenly like dropping where he was, curling up on the mat and giving himself totally to sleep. He could not recall when he had felt so tired, even on maneuvers. I wonder what kind of hell I'd catch from that little old Irisher of mine if she opened the front door and fell over me.

He was still grinning when he unlocked the door and stepped into the dark hall and felt a cold something press into the skin behind his ear and heard a spinning sort of voice behind him say, "Freeze, cop."

It's got to be I'm dreaming. I did fall asleep out there. This can't be for real. Not my house, Ellen, Bibby.

"Don't do it," the spinning voice said. "I just as soon shoot the top of your head off." It turned in another direction. "See if he's heeled."

Malone heard someone say, "Where's my wife and daughter?"

"Just stand still, fuzz." The muzzle dug in.

Rough hands ran up his body. Another man, a strong one. The hand scraped his left nipple and found the butt of the revolver sticking out of his shoulder holster, the one he used off duty. The hand came out and he felt lighter, lost.

"I got it," a second voice said. This one was as rough as the hands, but muted, a gargly purr like a cougar's.

"Put the lights on," the first voice said. It sounded happy. "Let me have it, Hinch."

Hinch.

"Just a minute, Fure."

Fure?

The lights went up. The first thing Malone saw through the archway was Ellen in the parlor perched like a Sunday school kid on the edge of her mother's New England rocker. She still had her coat on. Her face was the color of milk with the butterfat skimmed off.

"Can I move my head?" Malone asked.

"Like a good little cop." The spinny one.

Malone moved his head and came to life. The two men were wearing masks. If they had meant to kill they would not have cared if he and Ellen saw their faces. He let his breath out.

The masks were ridiculous. They were fullface and skintight, brown bear faces. The bear face on the little man was too big for him; it was wrinkled up like something unwrapped after a thousand years. The big man's fitted. The little one was a fashion plate. The big one was strictly motorcycle mugg, a hard case.

They go to the trouble of wearing masks and then they say each other's names out loud. Don't ever take chances with the dumb ones, John said; they either panic like animals or they like it.

The man called Fure liked it. He was now holding two guns, his own and Malone's. His was a seven-inch automatic, a foreign handgun. At first Malone thought it was a Mauser. But then he saw that it was a Walther PPK, a gun popular with continental law officers. Must be stolen. There had been nothing European in either voice.

That's the gun they killed Tom Howland with. The gun the little guy killed Howland with. It would have to be the little guy. He digs guns.

Fure was digging Malone's gun. The eyes behind the bear mask were crazy with joy. He had the Walther in his left armpit now and he was turning Malone's revolver over and over in his gloved hands.

"A Colt Trooper, Hinch. Six-shot, .357 Magnum. You ought to feel the balance of this baby. You're a pal, fuzz. Here." He handed the Walther to the big man. "Where's the ammo belt goes with this?"

"I don't keep it in the house—" Malone stopped. Fure was laughing. He reached into the hall closet and straightened up dangling the ammunition belt. The holster was empty, the bullet holders were full. "Naughty, naughty. Okay, fuzz. Inside with wifie."

Malone went into the parlor, his own gun digging into his head.

"Not near her. On that sofa over there."

Ellen's eyes followed him each inch of the way, saying do something, don't do anything.

He's a shrewd bugger for all his dumbness. He figures that together we're strong, apart we're helpless. Malone felt the rage rising. He sat down on the sofa.

"Ellen. Where's Bibby?"

"Upstairs with the woman."

"Is she all right?"

"I don't know. I think. I found them here when I got home. They won't even let me see her."

The woman. Then there were three of them. Apparently Ed Taylor had not seen the woman. Making it tougher for John and the state boys. They're looking for just two males.

"Your kid's okay for now, Malone," Fure said. He was running his hand over the Colt as if it were alive. "You

34

want her to stay that way you jump up and roll over. Hinch. The bag."

Hinch reached behind the sofa and came up with the black bag. He handed it to the fashion plate. It seemed to Malone that he did it very slowly.

"It's yours." The bag landed in Malone's lap. Fure scraped Ellen's treasured antique crewel chair over to him, the one with the shaky legs, and dropped into it. He kept fondling the Colt. They had to turn their heads to face him.

"What do I do with this, Fure?" Malone asked.

"Mr. Furia to cops."

"Mr. Furia."

"Take a look inside."

Malone unzipped the bag. Bundles of greenbacks stared up at him.

The purr behind him said, "I still think—"

"Just don't, Hinch," Furia said. "Know where this loot comes from, cop?"

"I can guess." Malone said in a soft voice. "You don't know about this, Ellen. Tom Howland was killed tonight at the Aztec plant and the payroll stolen. That's what all the excitement was about. This is the Aztec payroll. Right, Furia?"

"*Mister* Furia."

"Mr. Furia."

"Right."

He thought Ellen was going to topple over.

"Can I go to my wife, please? She looks sick."

"No."

Ellen's eyes were begging him. They made a quick upward roll toward where little Barbara was. "I'm all right, Loney."

Malone said, "What did you mean, this is mine?"

"You'll never have so much bread in your hands your whole life. Enjoy it."

"What did you mean?"

"Like for the time being."

"I don't get it."

"No? You're putting me on."

"I don't get any of this."

"You want I should spell it out? What you do, cop, is you hold this for us. Like you're a bank."

Malone tried to look stupid.

"You still don't get it," Furia said. "We drew a real dumb one, Hinch, a dummy town cop."

Hinch heehawed.

"Okay, dummy, listen good," Furia said. "With the bread on us we can't get through the roadblocks. Without it we can. They'll have no reason to handle us different from anybody else. Specially seeing there's going to be four of us in the car."

"Four of you," Malone said. His mouth was sticky. "I thought there were three."

"Four," Furia said. "Me, Hinch, Goldie, and your kid. Only she'll be Goldie's. Her mama, like."

"No," Ellen said. "*No.*"

"Yeah," Furia said. "Your kid's our receipt for the loot. All clear?"

"It's taking chances," Malone said carefully. "Suppose one of the officers recognizes her when you're stopped? This is a small town. Everybody knows everybody. That blows it."

"You better pray it don't. Can you pray?"

"Yes," Malone said. He wondered if it was true. He had not been inside a church since his confirmation. Ellen took Barbara every Sunday to the second mass, she's not going to grow up a heathen like you, Loney Baloney, you're a cross he has to bear Father Weil says.

"They tell me it helps," Furia said. One of the eyes in the bear mask winked. "All clear now?"

"All clear," Malone said.

"It better be. You try any cop stuff, dummy, or your missus there sets up a squawk, and the kid gets it through the head. Be a nice dummy and keep your old lady's yap shut and you get the kid back with her noggin in one piece. It's that simple."

Ellen's eyes were scurrying about and Malone said, "Ellen."

"I won't. They can't!"

"They can and you will. We have no choice, honey."

"You listen to your papa, honey," Furia said. "He's a smart dummy."

"How do we know they'll keep their word?" Ellen screamed. "You know what you've always said about kidnapers, Loney!"

"This isn't a kidnaping except technically. All they want is to hold Bibby as security till they can get the payroll back."

36

"We'll never see her again."

"They'll keep their word," Malone said. "Or they'll never see this money again. I'll make sure of that." He said to Furia, "All right, we have a deal. But now you listen to me and you listen good."

"Yeah?" Furia said.

"You hurt my daughter and I'll hunt you down and cut you to pieces. If it takes the rest of my life. You, and this goon, and that woman upstairs."

A growl behind him. "Fure, let me. Let me."

"You close your goddam mouth, Hinch!" Furia shouted. He jumped up and sprang forward, eyes in the wrinkled mask boiling. "I ought to knock you off right now, cop, you know that?"

"You need me," Malone said. He tried not to swallow.

"I ain't going to need you forever. Nobody talks to me like that. But nobody!"

"Remember what I said."

Their eyes locked. I could jump him now. And get a bullet in my back from the goon. And leave Ellen and Bibby to their mercy. Malone looked away.

"Goldie!" Furia yelled.

A woman's voice from upstairs said, "Yes, Fure."

"Wake the kid up and get her dressed!"

"Let me," Ellen whimpered. "Please? She'll be so scared."

"Let her," Malone said. "She's not going to try anything."

"She damn well better not." Furia waved the Colt. Ellen jumped to her feet and ran up the stairs.

Furia sat himself down on the rocker. The Colt was aimed at Malone's navel. He'd love to pull that trigger. He'd pull, not squeeze. He's kill-crazy. Malone looked down at his own hands. They were gripping the edge of the sofa so hard the knuckles resembled dead bone. He put his hands on the black bag.

They appeared at the top of the stairs, Ellen clutching Barbara's hand, the woman strolling behind them. The woman was wearing a mask, too. Through the mouth slit she was smoking a goldtipped cigaret. That was all Malone saw of her.

He said with a smile, "Baby. Come down here."

She was still sleepy. Ellen had dressed her in her best outfit, the red corduroy dress, the patent leather shoes, the blue wool coat and hat.

37

"Have you told her anything, Ellen?"

"What could I tell her?" Ellen said. "What?"

"Are we going someplace, daddy?" Bibby asked.

He set the black bag on the sofa and took her on his lap. "Bibby, are you all waked up?"

"Yes, daddy."

"Will you listen to me very, very hard?"

"Yes, daddy."

"These people are going to take you somewhere in a car. You're to go with them like a good girl."

"Aren't you and mommy going, too?"

"No, baby."

"Then why do I have to go?"

"I can't explain now. Let's say it's because I ask you to."

Her lips began to quiver. "I don't like them. Why are they wearing those masks? They're hor'ble."

"Oh, they're just pretending something."

"They have guns. They'll hurt me."

"I have a gun and I've never hurt you, have I?"

"No, daddy . . ."

"Come on," Furia said. "Time's up, like the screws say."

"Wait a minute, Fure," the woman said. "Let him explain it to his little girl."

"They won't hurt you, Bibby. I promise. Have I ever broken a promise to you?"

"No . . ."

"Remember, they won't hurt you. And you do whatever they tell you, Bibby. Whatever. You may even have to pretend, too, the way you did in the school play."

"Pretend what?" Barbara asked in an interested voice.

"Well, the chances are some policemen are going to stop the car. If they do you make believe you're sleeping in the lady's lap. If they wake you up and ask you questions, just say the lady is your mama and that's all."

"My mama? That lady?" She looked at her mother. Her mother looked at her.

"It's just pretend, baby. Do you understand?"

"I understand, but not *why*."

"Some day I'll explain the whole thing to you. But for now you've got to promise me you'll do whatever they say. Promise?"

"All right. When will they bring me back?"

"Oh, I don't know. A day, maybe two."

"Well," Barbara said. "I don't like to, but I guess I will. Goodbye, daddy." She held her face up to be kissed. Valentine face. He kissed it. She jumped off his lap and ran to her mother.

Ellen held on to her.

"Okay, okay," Furia said. Malone could have sworn he was grinning under the mask. "Let's get the show on the road, like they say."

"Ellen," Malone said.

The woman walked over and pulled Barbara from Ellen's clutch. Sexy figure, flashy getup, hard voice—maybe late twenties, though it was hard to tell without a face to go by. And brains, she's the brains. I know her from somewhere. I've heard that voice before. A long time ago.

"Come on, honey," the woman said. "We'll have just buckets of fun." She took Barbara's hand. "Fure. It won't hurt to buy insurance. With Barbara in the car, and you and her and me making like one happy family, it will look better if Hinch isn't with us. That getup of his doesn't go with the act."

"What, what?" Hinch said.

"Goldie's right," Furia said. "You hoof it, Hinch. You can cut off that main road into the woods somewheres and stand a good chance of not even being stopped. If they stop you, so what? One guy on the hitch. Stow your mask in the car. Also the heater—I'll drop it in the river before we get to the checkpoint. We'll meet you at the shack."

Hinch glanced at the Walther automatic in his hand. He's not used to guns. Malone tucked the observation away. "If you say so, Fure. Not because of her."

"I say so."

"Goldie and you and the kid'll meet me?"

"You worried about something?"

"Who, me? I ain't worried, Fure."

"Then do like I say. All right, Goldie."

The woman immediately said, "We'll be seeing you soon, mommy. Won't we, Bibs?" and they marched out through the archway and into the hall and out the front door and, incredibly, were gone.

Furia backed his way out. At the door he said, "Remember, cop, that's your kid we got. So don't be a hero."

And he was gone, too.

They were left alone with the black bag.

Standing at the window watching the Chrysler back

around and straighten out and head down Old Bradford Road toward Lovers Hill.

Standing at the window until the sound of the Chrysler died.

Then Ellen whirled and said in a voice full of hate, "You great big policeman you. You cowardly sonofabitch, you let them take my Bibby away. You *let* them!" and she was punching his chest and sobbing and he put his arms around her and said in a hoarseness of baffled rage, "Ellen, they won't hurt her, I'll kill them, they want that money more than anything, don't cry, Ellen, I'll get her back."

Thursday

The Child

Malone spent the first two hours trying to get Ellen to go to bed. She just sat in the rocker rocking. He kept at it like a gung ho D.I. because he could think of nothing else. Finally Ellen said, "How can I sleep when my baby is in the hands of those murderers?" and he gave up.

At one thirty Malone said, "Would you like some coffee?"

"I'll make some."

"No, I'll do it. You sit there."

"I don't want any."

"Watch the bag."

"What?"

"The bag. With the money."

She stared at it with loathing. It was on the coffee table before the sofa. "How much is in it?"

"I don't know. A week's payroll for Aztec."

"Count it," Ellen said. "I want to find out how much my child's life is worth."

"Ellen."

"It's like an insurance policy, isn't it?" Ellen said. "And

I've been after you for years to take one out for Bibby."
She laughed. "For her college education."

"Ellen, for God's sake."

"I know, we can't afford it. Can we afford it now? Oh,
never mind. Go drink your coffee."

"I only thought—"

"All *right*. I'll have some, too."

He hurried into the kitchen and put the kettle on to
boil. When he came back she was counting the money.

"Over twenty-four thousand dollars."

He looked at it.

"It's a lot of money," Malone said inanely.

Ellen grinned. "She's a lot of little girl."

He crammed the money back into the bag with trembling hands.

Neither took more than a few sips.

She kept rocking.

At three A.M. she suddenly said, "Is this all you're going
to do, Loney? Sit here?"

"What else can I do? There's nothing I can do tonight."

"What kind of a man are you? I thought I knew you."
Her eyes summed him up like an obituary.

"That little one, Furia," Malone explained to the floor.
"He's gun-happy. I want them to get to wherever they're
holing up without any trouble. It's the best protection
Bibby can have. They'll have no excuse ... Look, why
don't we talk in the morning? You're dead for sleep."

"Look who's talking."

"I'll go to bed in a while. Let me give you a pill."

"No."

"What good are you going to do Bibby sitting up all
night? You'll need your strength."

"And you won't?"

"I'll go, too, I tell you. Come on, how about it?"

At a quarter of four she allowed him to give her one of
the sleeping pills left over from Dr. Levitt's prescription,
when she had had the last miscarriage. She undressed
stiffly. She moved like Barbara's walking doll. He tucked
her into bed and stooped to kiss her.

She turned her face away.

He dragged back down to the parlor.

He carried the coffee things into the kitchen, washed
and dried them, put them away.

Then he went back upstairs.

The robe and slippers were on the gilt chair. Little

pajamas on the floor, the ones with the daisies she was ape over. He picked them up and folded them and hung them with care over the foot of her canopy bed. She loved her bed, with its lace-trimmed tester. It was a cheap one, everything they owned was cheap except a few of Ellen's mother's things, but Bibby was crazy about it. Her homework was on the worktable, in her hentrack handwriting. She always gets U-for-Unsatisfactory in Neatness. He picked up her plaid schoolbag and looked in. It was full of drawing papers, crayons of fun trees, happy cows, sunny houses, huge suns. E-for-Excellent in Art. Her drawings laughed, her teacher said.

Those killer skunks.

The sheet and blanket were flung back from when Ellen had awakened her. The pillow still showed the dent of her head.

He felt the bed, trying to feel his child.

But it was cold.

He eased the door to Barbara's room shut and looked in on his wife. Ellen was asleep. One arm was drawn across her face to shut the world out. She was making mewing sounds. Poor Ellen. Who else has she got to blame? She's got to get back at somebody.

He went downstairs again. He opened the black bag and counted out the money on the coffee table. $24,-358.25. It was like counting out Bibby. Is this all my kid is worth? Figure a life expectancy of seventy years. That makes her worth less than $350 a year.

Not enough. I'll kill them.

He fell asleep on the sofa, the black bag hugged to his belly.

He was driving the Pontiac along the river road through pearly fog at a hundred miles an hour leaving a sand wake like a launch and John Secco was sobbing, "Ease up, Wes, for God's sake take it slower, you'll kill us both, that's an order," but he kept his foot on the accelerator and he was grinning because the black Chrysler was right there up ahead. He could see its red lights through the fog and Bibby's face in the rear window frightened to death and the gold woman blowing cigaret smoke in her little white face. He stepped harder trying to push the pedal through the floor but no matter how hard he pushed the Chrysler kept the same distance ahead. Then it was rising in the air

44

in an arc like a flying fish heading for the Tonekeneke's black water and he tried to pull it back with both hands to keep it from falling into the river but he had no strength, it slipped through his fingers and the splash hit him like a stone wall and he found his voice Bibby *Bibby BIBBY* ...

He opened his eyes.

Ellen was kneeling by the sofa with her arms around him.

"Loney, wake up. You're having a dream."

He sat up. His belly felt sore. It was the bag digging into him.

"Oh, Loney, I'm sorry."

"About what?" He was shaking.

"The way I acted last night." Ellen's arms tightened. "As if it's your fault. I'm a bitch."

"No, you're not." He kissed the top of her head.

"Forgive me?"

"What's to forgive?" He swung his legs to the floor and groaned. "I swear I'm tireder now than I was last night. No calls?"

"No, darling. She'll be all right. I know she will."

"Of course she will."

"Why didn't you get undressed and into bed? No wonder you're exhausted. This sofa is the original torture rack."

"I must have dropped off. I could use a couple gallons coffee, Mrs. Malone."

"It's all ready for you. You just sit here. I'll get it."

"No, I'll come into the kitchen. What time is it?"

"Seven thirty."

"I have to make a call."

She was instantly alarmed. "To where?"

"To the station."

"Loney, you promised—"

"Don't worry, Ellen."

They went into the kitchen. Ellen spooned out the coffee, watching him. He went to the wall phone and dialed.

"Wes Malone," Malone said. "Who's this?"

"Trooper Miller. Oh. Wes." The young Resident Trooper sounded groggy. "What can I do for you?"

"Chief Secco there?"

"He's gone home for some shuteye. Don't ask me why, but I volunteered to hold down the fort till the day man comes in. Where the hell is he? I haven't slept since night before last."

"What's doing? I mean about those killers."

"Not a thing. Looks like they slipped through before we set up the blocks. Anything I can do for you?"

"No. I was just wondering."

"Forget it. Somebody 'll pick 'em up somewhere. Chief says you're on a couple days' leave, Wes. Make love to your wife or something. No rest, but it's recreation."

Miller hung up, chuckling.

Malone hung up.

He turned to find Ellen standing over the cups with the kettle poised, a human question mark.

"They got through, Ellen. So Bibby's okay."

I hope.

"Thank God."

Ellen poured. A silence dropped between them. He sat down at the kitchen table and set the black bag on the floor between his feet, where he could feel it.

When Malone came down from his shower Ellen was just cradling the phone.

"Who was that?"

"I called Miss Spencer."

"Who's she?"

"The school nurse, for the umpty-eleventh time. We have to have some excuse why Bibby won't be in school today, Loney. I said I was afraid she might be coming down with the flu and that I'd probably keep her home over the weekend just in case."

He touched her black Irish hair. "What would I do without you?"

"I'll bet you say that to all your girls."

"Yep." He kissed her and felt the tension of her body through the terry robe. "I'm one hell of a cop. I never even thought of the school."

"Oh, Loney, I've got to do something!" His stomach contracted. She was jerking with sobs again. "My baby ... waking up this morning with those horrible people ..."

"A few minutes ago you were thanking God they got through all right."

She kept sobbing. He kept stroking her. He could find nothing else to say. He had always hated to see Ellen cry,

46

he was a complete coward about her tears. They made him furious, they brought back memories of his mother, who had cried her eyes out when his father was alive. The night after his mother-in-law's funeral Ellen had cried till dawn, and he had run up and down in their bedroom finding no words of comfort, only curses at his helplessness.

"I'm sorry," Ellen pushed away from him. "Bawling isn't going to help Bibby."

"You cry all you want."

"No, sir. That nonsense is *over*. Let me make you some breakfast."

"I'm not hungry."

"You've got to. You hardly touched your dinner at the Inn last night, you were so tired."

"I'd throw it right back at you," Malone said. "Look, hon. We've got to figure out where we stand."

"All right, Loney." She immediately sat down. They both avoided the empty third chair.

"There's got to be something we can do besides stay here like bumps on a log."

"Let's get settled first on what we *can't* do," Ellen said. "What we can't do is let Chief Secco or anybody know they were here last night and took Bibby. That's the one thing I won't let you do, Loney. We'd better have an understanding about that right off."

"What do you think I am, crazy?"

"Loney, look at me."

He looked at her.

"You're not a cop in this thing. You're Bibby's father."

"I told you," he said gruffly.

"Just remember," Ellen said. "Or I swear on my child's life I'll walk out on you and you'll never see me again."

"What do you want," he shouted, "my blood?"

"Loney. I had to say it. We have to have that clear."

"All right, so it's clear! She's my child, too, remember!"

"Don't be mad at me, Loney."

"All right." He reached down and brought up the black bag and set it on the table between them. He stared at it bitterly. "We don't even know what they look like. Those goddam masks."

"Yes," Ellen said. "Goldilocks and the Three Bears."

"Huh?"

"Didn't you notice?"

"Notice what?"

47

"The woman was wearing a Goldilocks mask. The little one—Furia—he was wearing the Papa Bear mask, and the big bruiser was wearing the Mama Bear one. It must be a set."

"Then there's a Baby Bear mask! For Bibby?"

"That's what I'm wondering."

He jumped up, sat down again, shook his head. "No, that wouldn't make sense. Why would they put a mask on her? It wouldn't serve any purpose."

"I just thought I'd mention it," Ellen said.

He sat thinking. She got up and refilled their cups. "We can do one of two things, Ellen. We can either sit here and wait—"

"I'd *die*."

"Or I can try to find their hideout and get Bibby back."

"Wouldn't that be terribly dangerous for Bibby?"

"Could be."

"Oh, God."

"Ellen. Why don't I try? I can size up the situation better if and when I find out where they're hiding. If I see it's too dangerous for Bibby I won't move a muscle. How does that sound to you?"

"If you're sure. How can you be sure?"

"Then, if I can get Bibby safely away, we can turn the payroll over to John and tell him the whole story."

"And have those three come after us in revenge?" Ellen said with a shudder. "Forget about John, Loney."

"This money belongs to Aztec. We can't just let them walk off with it. I mean of course first we get Bibby back—"

"That's what I was afraid of. You're being a cop again."

"I'm *not*."

"Let them have the money. As long as we get Bibby back. Maybe the best thing after all is to sit here and wait. They'll come back with Bibby and we'll hand over the bag and that will be that."

"And maybe that won't be that," Malone said. "I won't kid you, Ellen. We've got to face up to the facts. If we do what you say—wait for them to bring Bibby back and pick up the money—all three of us stand a good chance of getting shot. That Furia would get a kick out of it. Why should he leave us alive? Even if we didn't see their faces, we've heard their voices and we know their names. Hoods like that must have a record somewhere—I think Furia's served time, he used the word 'screw,' which is a prison term for 'guard'—they can probably be identified through the FBI central file in a matter of hours. They can't be that dumb—I'm pretty sure the woman isn't. And they're already in the bag for one murder. No, we can't trust them, Ellen. We've got to take some kind of action. Try *something*."

Ellen's face had gone the color of skim milk again. "All right then, Loney, you find their hideout the way you said. If you can rescue Bibby we can go off somewhere, hide or something, till those monsters are caught."

Malone got up and went over to the kitchen sink to look out the window. But he was not seeing the dirt driveway. When he turned around his eyes had come back. "It might not be so tough at that, Ellen. Actually when you think about it we have quite a few leads to where they're holed up. Furia told Hinch to walk there, so how far can it be? And it's likely somewhere across The Pike on the way out of town or they'd have been able to get there without worrying about being stopped at a checkpoint. On top of everything, the little punk mentioned woods and a shack."

"Balsam Lake," Ellen breathed.

"That's how it figures to me. If it's a Lake cabin—"

"They must have broken into one of them."

He shook his head, fighting his way through the mush. "That would be leaving a lot to luck. This wasn't set up that way, Ellen. It's been planned well in advance. I didn't mention it, but John says Tom Howland must have been in on the robbery and they doublecrossed him at the last minute. That would mean previous contacts between the robbers and Howland. That means they've been in town before. Also, the woman sounded familiar to me. I know I've heard her voice, a long time ago, I think. I'm betting she comes from New Bradford. Which could be why they picked it for their robbery in the first place, because she knows the town. Anyway, it all adds up to preparation. If they prepared everything else, they'd prepare a hideout too. Maybe months ago."

"A rental?"

"Why not? They could have rented one of the cabins, even used it during the summer. So if the police come nosing around the cabin now, what have they got to be afraid of? Of course, they'd rather nobody knew, but if they can produce a lease—"

49

"But in November, Loney? Nobody's at the Lake in November."

"That's not so. A few people from downstate rent cabins by the year—use them for weekends after the summer season. We patrol that Lake road the year round."

Ellen was considering his argument stubbornly. "I don't know. It sounds too dumb to me. I mean robbing and killing and still planning to hide out for any length of time within walking distance of where they did it. It seems to me that's the last thing they'd do."

"And maybe that's just why they did it," Malone insisted. "Who'd think of looking for them practically on the scene of the crime? The more I think about it the more I'm sure we've got something. I'm going to find that cabin, Ellen. Do you feel up to staying here alone while I scout around? I don't think they'll try coming back before dark."

"Don't worry about me. Do you think you can locate it in one day, Loney? There's an awful lot of cabins around Balsam Lake."

"I'm not starting at the Lake. I'm starting in town."

"What do you mean?"

"If they rented a cabin, it had to be through a real estate agent."

"Loney, be careful! You'll get people suspicious asking questions."

"Not if I do it right. I wish to hell I knew how the real pros go about a thing like this."

"Just keep remembering Bibby. Please, Loney?"

She clung to him, begging with her whole body. He kissed her and pulled away. She remained in the kitchen doorway.

Malone went upstairs. As he was rummaging through the clothes closet in their bedroom he suddenly remembered his hunting rifle. He had not used it in years. Had they searched the upstairs before he got home last night and found it? Ellen might have forgotten to mention it.

It was still on the top shelf of the closet, wrapped in oil rags.

He took it down and unwrapped it. After all this time not a speck of rust. That was one thing the Marines had taught him, how to take care of a weapon. With the rifle in his hands the tiredness was rubbed out. He felt around

50

on the shelf and found the boxes of .22 long-rifle cartridges.

You pulled a boner, *Mister* Furia.

He could have shouted with joy.

But he stood there, weighing and sorting. As he weighed and sorted the tiredness came back.

Not with Bibby in their hands. And a .22 wasn't much. You could kill a rabbit or a fox with it, but a rabbit or a fox wasn't a man with a Colt Trooper and a Walther automatic. I wish I could have afforded that .303 at the discount store. But the shells for it came to five-six dollars a box. Or that M-1 carbine they had on sale.

"Loney, what are you doing up there?"

He rewrapped the rifle and stowed it along with the cartridges at the rear of the shelf and went out into the hall to the linen closet and got some bathmats and went back and covered the gun and ammunition.

He changed into sneakers and put on his oilstained green-and-black plaid hunting jacket and cap and went back downstairs. Ellen was still standing in the kitchen doorway.

"What were you doing up there?"

"Don't let that bag out of your sight," Malone said, and left.

Malone drove the Saab off The Pike a few hundred yards north of the cloverleaf into the gravel driveway past the gilded white sign T. W. HYATT & SON REAL ESTATE and pulled up before the one-story frame building. It was his fourth stop of the morning.

He went in.

"Hi, Edie."

"Well, if it isn't the lawman," Edie Golub said, looking up from her typewriter. There was a pencil stuck in her dead-black-dyed hair. "Don't shoot, Officer, I'll come quietly." She was one of the girls from high school who wouldn't give him the time of day. She had never married. "Don't you ever crack a smile, Wes?"

"I'm off duty, I guess I can risk it," Malone said, smiling. "Young Tru in?" Old Tru had retired the year before and taken his grouch and arthritis to St. Petersburg, Florida. The whole town had breathed out. He had always been the one who stood up in town meeting and threw a monkey wrench into the works.

51

"He's going through the mail." She got up and opened the door to the inner office. "It's Wes Malone, Mr. Hyatt. Can you see him?"

"Wes? Sure thing!" Young Tru sounded eager.

Here we go again.

Malone went in. Hyatt was waiting with his best sales smile. He was a tall thin man with a badly pockmarked face, dressed as always like an *Esquire* ad. He was one of New Bradford's ladies' men, big on church socials and parties, the last one home. He was supposed to have been sleeping with Edie Golub for years—he had an old black leather couch in his office—with her "Mr. Hyatts" in the presence of third parties as their coverup.

"Sit down, Wes, park it. How's the manhunt going?"

"Oh, they got away." It was the fourth time he had had to say it.

"I understand Tom Howland was in on it up to his fat ass."

"Where did you hear that?" It was impossible to keep a secret in New Bradford.

"It's all over town," Hyatt said. "I heard it in the bank a few minutes ago. Is it true, Wes?"

"I wouldn't know. I went off duty before the case broke. Tell you what I dropped in for, Tru—"

"I knew that outfit would get shlogged some day," Hyatt said. "Whoever heard of a company in this day and age still paying their help in cash? If they'd invest a few bucks in a modern bookkeeping system—with an honest bookkeeper, ha-ha!—put in one of those computers, pay off in checks ... But I guess they got a big inventory in pay envelopes."

"You're right, Tru, they asked for it all right," Malone said. "Oh, what I'm here for. We've been having a little trouble over at the Lake. Now that the season is over some kids have been going down there nights to booze it up and generally raise hell—they've broken into a few cabins—and we've had some complaints from people who lease by the year. I've been getting up a list of the year-round renters to make sure we don't miss any. You know how some people are, afraid to make a complaint. Did you place any one-year rentals at the Lake in, say, the past six-seven months, Tru?"

"I don't think so. Bob Doerr gets most of the Lake stuff. Did you try Bob?"

"I got a few names from him. Well, I won't keep you."

There was only one real estate office in town he had not covered. If I strike out at Taugus Realty . . .

"No, wait a minute," Hyatt said.

He sat still.

"Now that I think of it, I seem to recall there was one. Edie?"

She popped her hairdo in. "Yes, Mr. Hyatt?"

"Didn't we write a lease for one of the Lake cabins around May, June, somewhere around there?"

"I really don't remember."

"Well, look it up, will you?" Hyatt sat back. "Y'know, Wes, I can never figure you out."

Find it Edie.

"What have I done now, Tru?"

"Here you are off duty and you're working. What are you, bucking for John's job? Don't you ever relax?"

"I guess I'm not the relaxing type."

Find it Edie.

"That's the thing with you married suckers. You don't know how to live. Now you take me."

"The way I hear it," Malone said dutifully, "you've been taken by experts."

"Who, me? The hell you say! Who said that?"

"Here it is, Mr. Hyatt." Edie Golub had a lease in her hand. Malone watched it all the way across the rug. Hyatt took it from her, and she stood there. But when he stared up at her she left quickly, shutting the door with a bang.

"Yes, this is the one. Somebody named Pratt, William J. Pratt. Signed the lease May twenty-third. How's that for a memory? You want to see this, Wes?"

"If you don't mind." Malone took the lease as casually as he could manage. William J. Pratt typed in. The signature unreadable. Deliberately so, he was positive, a disguised handwriting. It had to be a phony!

For Hyatt's benefit he produced a list and added the name and location of the cabin to it. He could have found it with his eyes shut. He could taste it. He handed the lease back and rose. "Thanks a lot, Tru. I'll check this one out with the others."

Hyatt waved. "Think nothing of it."

The real estate man went back to his mail, still a little miffed. Malone jumped for the Saab.

The description on the lease placed the cabin at the southeast end of Balsam Lake where it narrowed to muddy shallows. It was the least desirable section of the Lake.

According to Malone's list, "Pratt's" rental was the only one in this scattered cabin area that extended beyond the summer season. Made to order for a post-season hideout.

He drove off the blacktop into a lane, little more than a dirt path, and cached the Saab behind a clump of diseased birch trees in a thicket of wild huckleberry bushes. The bushes were nearly bare, but they made a tall tangle and they camouflaged most of the car. He draped fallen evergreen branches over the parts that showed, and when he was satisfied that the Saab was effectively hidden he left on foot.

He was a mere three hundred yards from the cabin, but his approach took the better part of a half hour. After a few yards he got down on his belly. It was the Marine game of his boyhood over again, traveling on hips and elbows, never raising his head above the underbrush, avoiding dried-out branches, sticking where he could to the cushioning ground pine. He made so little noise that once he surprised a squirrel on the ground; he could have killed it with a stone.

At last Malone reached the clearing.

He did not enter it. The clearing had been hacked in a rough circle out of a thick stand of pine woods and along its perimeter wild azalea, laurel, and sumac had taken root in an almost continuous band of bush. Here Malone settled himself.

He had a good view of the cabin. There were some expensive handhewn log structures along the Lake, but most of the cottages were of cheap clapboard or shingle construction, labeled "cabins" by the Balsam Lake Properties Association, whose brochures leaned heavily toward fiction. The "Pratt" cabin was a slapped-together shack of green-painted shingle walls streaked with years of damp. It had a badly weathered shake roof and a midget open porch with two sagging steps. The power line that provided its electricity dropped in from above the woods and hooked onto a naked insulator attached to the outside of the house. A bluish haze seeped out of the tin chimney on the roof. Like all the Lake cottages it used propane gas for cooking; Malone could see the silvered tank at the side of the cabin.

The haze coming out of the tin vent told Malone what he wanted to know.

The cabin was occupied.

They were there.

Malone had been lying in the bushes for almost two hours—he had just looked at his watch, it was half-past noon—when the door of the cabin opened and a man stepped out. He was not wearing a mask but his face was in shadow and Malone could not make out the features. He was sorry now that he had not stopped in town to pick up a pair of binoculars or at least borrow a pair from Jerry Sampson at the drug store, well it was too late for that. The man was a very big man with very heavy shoulders and Malone knew he was the one the small man had called Hinch.

The man looked around and then he jumped off the porch and strolled toward the woods east of the cabin. Malone got a good look at him in the sun. He was wearing a black leather jacket and tight black pants and blue Keds, and he had red hair that bushed down over his bull's neck. He had a broken nose and a face that went with it, brutal and stupid.

Here's one guy I'd better stay out of his reach. He'd stomp me to death and not even breathe hard.

Malone stopped thinking and started tracking.

He slid back on his belly until he was protected by the trees and then he got up in a crouch and keeping to the ground pine made a rapid quarter circle to the east, traveling on his toes. He knew where Hinch was headed, the other dirt road that led to the cabin. They must have their car hidden there.

He was right. They had parked it off the road and made an attempt to hide it but it was clumsily done and Malone could see it from the bushes across the road. It was the black sedan, the Chrysler New Yorker, covered with dust.

Hinch was bulling around in the underbrush. He got to the trunk and unlocked it and dug in for something inside. When the hand reappeared it was holding a half gallon of whisky by the neck. The seal on the bottle looked intact. He closed the trunk lid and shambled back toward the clearing.

Malone backtracked. He was just in time to see Hinch step into the cabin and shut the door.

He settled himself in his original hiding place. It would be a long wait if they were starting on another bottle. He did not know exactly what he was waiting for. A chance. A break. Anything. They might not show at all. Or they might all get drunk and pass out. The whisky might do the trick. I'll have to see where I go from there.

I should have taken the rifle. Why did I chicken out? I could have shot this Hinch in the brush. From ten yards away even the measly .22 cartridge in the right spot would have taken him out for good.

Yes, and what would the other two do to Bibby when they heard a shot?

No. Wait them out.

If only they hadn't taken his revolver. There was always something reassuring about the Colt's weight on his hip, even though he had never fired it except on the state police pistol range during refreshers, and once at a marauding bobcat.

He could see Ellen's face. Waiting.

Ellen's face wavered, and Malone became aware of another, immediate danger.

His eyes insisted on drooping.

Those damned four days and nights on duty, and that heavy cold before that. The couple hours' sleep I got last night were an appetizer, worse than nothing. He began to fight the droop.

His eyes kept doing it.

He fought them desperately. He pushed them up with his fingers. But even holding them open did no good. The clearing shimmered, fogged over.

If they're drinking in there they're maybe frightening Bibby. Don't be scared, baby. Daddy's coming.

The sky began to swing like Bibby's swing in the backyard. Up . . . down . . .

If I maybe shut my eyes for just a few seconds.

Bibby I'm out here. It won't be long.

He was still talking to her when sleep washed everything out.

"No more," Furia said. He took the bottle from Hinch and screwed back the top. Hinch was left with a few drops in his glass.

"Aw, Fure," Hinch said.

"I said that's enough." Furia was not drinking. He never drank anything but soda pop, not even beer. You're scared to let go Goldie once told him, laughing.

"Okay, Fure, okay." Hinch upended the glass and let the drops trickle into his mouth. He tossed the glass into the sink. It hit some dirty dishes and shattered.

"Watch it," Furia said. "You'll wake up the kid. That's all we need is a bawling kid."

"She's out like a light," Goldie said. She was still nursing hers, her third; she knew there would not be a fourth, not with Fure around. "It's wonderful what a mouthful of booze will do to a nine-year-old. She's gone on a real long trip." She giggled. "Byebye Bibby."

"You could be sent up for feeding a kid the sauce," Hinch said with a grin. "You want to get sent up, Goldie?"

"Listen, buster, when I'm sent up it's going to be for something important," Goldie said. "Like for murder?"

"All right, all right," Furia said. "You better get going, Hinch."

"Yes, *sir*," Hinch said.

"And don't go getting smart, Hinch. Just do like I told you. You remember what you got to do?"

"What am I, a birdbrain? Sure I remember. Hang around town, keep my ears open. Right, Fure?"

"That's right. Nothing else. No more booze, no picking up a broad, no anything. Just listen. And don't call attention to yourself."

"The best place to hear the dirt is Freight Street," Goldie said. "That's the street that runs past the railroad station. The old town rummies hang out down there. Cash their social security checks and run to the liquor store. Buy a bottle of cheap port, Hinch, and pass it around. They'll tell you what's going on. They get the word before the Selectmen do. You can park the car in the railroad lot. Everybody uses it."

"Yes, *ma'am*," Hinch said, and started for the door.

"Wait a minute. I'm going with you. We can meet afterward at the lot."

"The hell you say." Furia banged on the table with the bottle. "You're going no place, Goldie!"

"Will you listen to me?" Goldie said wearily. "Before you blow your stack. I've got to get a few things."

"Like what?"

"Like Tampax, for one, if you must know. I fell off the roof this morning. Also I need hair dye, I'm starting to sprout green around the roots. And some deodorant for Hinch. I can't stand being around him any more. He stinks."

"I ain't heard no complaints from my broads," Hinch said hotly.

"Well, I'm not one of your broads. Why don't you

57

break down and take a bath once in a while? We need some groceries, too, Fure. Bread, and there's no milk for the kid."

Furia considered this.

Hinch spat into the sink. "I thought you were the one so scared to show your pussy around here."

"You're sore because I wouldn't put out for you," Goldie said, smiling.

Furia went up to Hinch and stuck his jaw out. The top of his head came to Hinch's chin. "You been making passes at Goldie?"

Hinch backed off. "Fure, I never! I swear to God. She's just trying to get me in trouble. She don't like me."

"And that's a fact," Goldie said, still smiling.

"You lay one finger on her, Hinch, and you know what? You're dead."

"I never," Hinch mumbled.

"Just remember I gave you the word. About going, Goldie, the answer is no. It's too risky."

"It might be if I went to a beauty parlor. But there's a drug store in town that didn't use to be here. And I noticed a supermarket last night that's new, too. I'll be careful, don't worry."

"The hell with the milk," Furia said. "Nobody ever bought me no milk. I was lucky to get a glass of water without no cockaroach in it."

"Whatever you say, Fure."

"Tell you what, Goldie. Long as you're going, bring me back some of that frozen pizza pie crap. I feel like a pizza. And some cherry-vanilla ice cream."

"You'll go to hell in a hand basket," Goldie said, laughing. "Okay, pizza and ice cream."

"And say. Does this wide place in the road have a newspaper?"

"Sure, a weekly. Comes out on Thursdays."

"That's today. Groovy. Pick me up one." Furia chuckled. "I want to read my reviews."

Goldie nodded. She was in slacks and tight turtleneck and pea jacket, she had her hair bound in a scarf. She picked up her purse. "Okay, Stinkfoot, let's go. I'll stick my nose out the window."

"I swear to Christ," Hinch gargled, "if it wasn't for Fure I'd tear that bitch tongue of yours out by the roots."

"Then what would he play with?" Goldie said, and sailed past him as if he weren't there.

58

Malone awoke to pain. Something that felt like a needle was scratching his face and his back was one burning ache. For a moment he did not know where he was.

Then he remembered and he brushed the branch out of his face. He sat up in the darkness.

Dark.

He had slept all afternoon and into the evening, well into it. The moon was high. He could not see the hands of his watch but he knew it must be late. He had slept ten hours or more.

He stared over at the cabin. It was lit up; the shades were only half drawn. A figure passed, another. A third. They were careless. He could not see above their waists, but they were all there.

What chances have I missed?

How in God's name could I have let myself fall asleep with Bibby in there?

He strained to see her.

Bibby Bibby.

There's no sense to this.

There's no sense to me.

Malone crouched in his bush for ten minutes arguing with the prosecution. While he argued he found himself working his muscles, beginning with his feet and going up. Isometric exercises got the aches and stiffness out. It was something he had learned to do during the cramped hours in the patrol car.

He worked at it with passion.

It was like a miracle. When he was altogether limbered up he had a plan readymade. He did not know where it came from. One moment he was blundering about in a mystery, the next it was all clear, solved, perfect.

He began to crawl about in the dark, feeling for dry twigs, brittle leaves, pine needles. He arranged them just outside the clearing on a line of sight with the cabin's front windows, making a little pile of tinder in the heart of the brush and laying down thicker pieces of branch like the spokes of a wheel over it, Boy Scout fashion. It should be enough to blaze up and start a smoky fire. The bushes would burn slowly, it had been a wet month, there was not much danger of setting the woods on fire. But I'll burn the whole damn county down if it means getting Bibby out of there.

They're bound to see the fire or at least smell the smoke. They can't afford to have half of New Bradford roaring into the woods to put it out. They'll have to leave the shack and put it out themselves. If the woman stays inside I'll break her neck.

He blocked the view from the cabin with his body and on hands and knees struck a paper match and very carefully touched the flame to the tinder.

It flared up.

Malone ducked into the woods and made his way rapidly around the perimeter of the clearing to a point at right angles to the porch. Here he stopped. He had both the fire and the front door in sight. The fire had grown taller and huskier, it was jumping. Then the bushes began to smoke. The smoke tumbled into the clearing like a surf, a shifting wall through which the flames licked and darted. The sharp sweetness of burning leaves and green wood rolled through the clearing and struck the cabin. Malone's eyes began to water.

Come *on*.

They came. One of them opened the door and Malone heard a startled yell, then something about blankets, and a moment later three figures dashed out of the shack and across the clearing and began slapping the fire and stamping on embers, shouting orders to one another. They ran around like hooched-up Indians in a Western.

But Malone was not there to applaud. Even before they were at the fire he was on his way around to the back door of the cabin and yanking at the knob. The door was locked. He ran at it and through it without feeling anything. He found Barbara immediately. She was lying on a cot in a tiny bedroom with a door open to the kitchen and he ran in and snatched a blanket and wrapped her in it and flung her over his shoulder fireman style and ran out and through the broken door and into the woods and made a great circle around to where he had hidden the Saab and then he was on the dirt road and a heartbeat after that on the blacktop speeding away from the Lake.

Only then did the smell from the sleeping child's mouth register on his brain and he knew what they had done to her to keep her quiet.

Through the rage he kept telling himself well it could have been worse a lot worse I hope Ellen sees it that way goddam their slimy souls.

It was like a movie. One shot he was in the shack bundling Bibby in a blanket the next he was in the Saab

60

pushing it at its top speed and the next he was in his own parlor.

And there was Ellen, flying from the rocker, grabbing Bibby from him, sitting down with the child in her arms to rock her the way she used to when Bibby was an infant. And staring up at him with such fear in her eyes that he wondered if he wasn't dreaming.

"What is it, Ellen? What are you so scared about? Wake up, honey, I got Bibby back and she's okay, they gave her a shot of whisky to keep her quiet, that's why she's sleeping and smells like that but it won't hurt her, don't worry, maybe give her a headache tomorrow morning, that's all. Now you put her to bed while I call John to shoot some cars over to Balsam and pick those three hoods up," he could not seem to stop talking, something was terribly wrong, her eyes said so, and he didn't want to know, it was too much, he had had enough for one day, "and we'll give John the bag with the money——"

Ellen mouthed, "It isn't here any more."

Thursday—Friday

The Money

"What do you mean?" Malone said. "What do you mean it isn't here any more?"

"Somebody took it."

"Who? How? I told you not to let it out of your sight!"

"Don't yell at me, Loney. I don't think I can take any more."

"Will you answer me, for God's sake? How did it happen?"

Ellen got out of the rocker with Barbara. She pressed her lips to the child's defenseless neck. "After I've got this baby in bed."

He sank onto the sofa staring. Halfway up the stairs she turned. "Did you say whisky? They gave a nine-year-old *whisky*?"

He did not answer. She hissed something profane and vicious and ran the rest of the way.

Malone sat there listening to the small sounds from upstairs.

I got Bibby back. The money is gone. Now what?

His elbows dug into his dirt-soaked knees and he took his head in his hands and tried to think. But the thoughts were stuck, going round and round like a toy train.

When Ellen came down she was calmer. Give a woman her kid to tuck in and she doesn't give a damn about anything else. She took his cap off and got him out of his hunting jacket and smoothed his hair. "I'll get you some coffee."

Malone shook his head. "Now tell me what happened."

She sat down by his side and held on to her own hands.

"There's not an awful lot to tell, Loney. It happened so fast. I had to go to the bathroom this afternoon—"

"And you left the money in here?"

"What was I supposed to do, take the bag to the toilet with me? Why didn't you chain it to my wrist? How was I supposed to know—?"

"All *right*." He did a swiveling exercise with his head, making his neckbones creak. "I can't seem to get this tiredness out. I could be coming down with the flu."

"You're such an optimist. You could be fighting it off." She smiled at him, anxious to get away from the money. She didn't want to talk about it.

"You went to the toilet and you left the bag here in the parlor," Malone said. And he could think of nothing else. "You came out and it was gone?"

"No, he was still here."

"Who was still here?"

"The man—"

"What man? What did he look like?"

"I'll tell you if you'll only let me," Ellen said sullenly. "He must have heard me flush and realized I was coming out so he hid in the hall next to the bathroom door. I guess. Anyway, just as I stepped out something hit me on the head and I fell down."

"Hit you?" For the first time Malone saw the bruise. It was well up in her hair, a purple and yellow-green lump the size of a robin's egg. The hair around the lump was stiff with clotted blood. "Christ!"

He clutched her. She made a hard bundle in his arms.

"And I sounded off at you! We'd better get Dr. Levitt to look at your head right away."

"I don't need any doctor. It throbs like hell, that's all. The main thing, Loney, we've got Bibby back."

He cursed. He did not know whom or what he was cursing—the unknown thief, the punks, Tom Howland, himself, or fate. The main thing, yes, but it was not over, not by a long shot. Not with that money gone. They'd have real blood in their eyes this time.

"I don't get it," Malone said, trying to. "Who could it have been? Did you get a look at him, Ellen?"

"Barely, as I was falling. And then it was all in a blur, sort of. It's a wonder I saw anything at all. I don't even remember landing on the floor. I must have been out fifteen minutes."

"Can you give me a description? Did you see his face?"

"Not hardly. He was wearing something over his head."

He was startled. "One of those Three Bears masks?"

"No, it was a woman's stocking. You know, like they use in movie holdups. That they can see through, but you can't make out anything clear."

"Did you see what he hit you with?"

"No, but I found the pieces afterward," Ellen said grimly. "It was my St. Francis." Ellen's St. Francis had been given to her by her father's sister Sue, whose name became Sister Mary Innocent. It was a cheap ceramic, but Ellen prized it. "I tried to paste the pieces together with Epoxy glue, but there were too many little ones."

He knew what losing her St. Francis meant to her. Her aunt had died in a Bolivian mission, throat cut by a crazy bush Indian convert.

Crazy. This whole thing is crazy.

"Did you see anything else, Ellen? What about his clothes?"

"A jacket, pants."

"Anything else?"

She shook her head and he saw her wince. He clutched her tighter.

"How big was he?"

"I don't know. Not very big. I'm not sure of anything, Loney. It's like I saw it all in a dream."

"Did he say anything? Did you hear his voice?"

"No."

"It's one of those three."

It was Ellen's turn to be startled. She twisted in his arms.

"One of them doublecrossed the other two. It's got to be, Ellen, nothing else makes sense. I fell asleep in the bushes out there while I was spying on the cabin. I was so exhausted I slept the whole day. Any one of them could have gone into town and I wouldn't have seen. They could even have taken turns. It figures. Nobody else knew the money was here. And if he wasn't big, like you say, it couldn't have been that Hinch. So it looks like it was the gun-happy one, Furia. You didn't see or hear a car?"

"I told you, I was in the bathroom not paying attention. And afterward, by the time I came to, whoever it was was gone. I ran outside and there wasn't a soul on the street, no car, anything."

Malone was glaring at the carpet.

"What is it, Loney?"

"Listen, baby, I've got to tell you. We're in a worse spot than before."

"But we've got Bibby back," Ellen said, as if that wiped out everything. She pulled away and jumped up. "I think I'll go back up and see if she's all right."

He reached for her. "You don't understand—"

"I don't want to!" And that made a lot of sense, that did.

"You've got to. Will you please listen, honey? They'll be back for their blood money. They'll be mad as mad dogs because I got Bibby away from them, and when they find out the money's gone, too, our name is mud."

"But one of them took it! You said so yourself."

"You don't think he's going to admit it to the other two, do you? Ellen, you and Bibby are in terrible danger. I've got to get you both out of here fast. I'll phone John right now. You go on up and get Bibby awake and dressed—"

"You do and you're dead," said the spinning voice.

They filled the archway.

He had not heard them come in, they must move like cats after a nest, it was ridiculous, they didn't look dangerous, they looked like a corny act on TV, the little one in the neat suit, the bruiser in the leather jacket and sneakers, the blonde in slacks and pea jacket with a scarf of psychedelic colors hanging down her front, as freaky as some farout hippie combo and as unconvincing. Ridiculous.

But my revolver in Furia's mitt, that's not ridiculous, and the Walther automatic in Hinch's (so Gunslinger didn't throw it in the Tonekeneke after all, he couldn't bear to part with it), and the look behind the eyeslits in the girl's mask that's somehow worse than the guns—not ridiculous, no.

They were back in their masks again (why? was it for

making horrible faces like the kids make when they're feeling nasty, to get the upper hand through looking horrible, half in play, half serious?), but there was nothing playful about these three, Tom Howland found that out, so did Ed Taylor, and what game is little doublecrossing Furia going to play now?

I wish I could see his face.

Furia marched in and asserted himself from just outside Malone's reach. The Colt Trooper was doing a dance. Malone watched it, fascinated. The bobcat's tail had done that just before he shot it. I wish I had it now. Put a slug right between Papa Bear's eyes. And a lightning second shot at Mama Bear. He fought with his fantasy.

"There's one thing puts me uptight it's a wise-guy cop," Furia was saying. There was a thickness, a curdle, in his tight voice; Malone could almost taste the sludge. "You made a first-class monkey out of me, fuzz. Didn't you?"

"She's my kid," Malone said. "What would you do if it was your kid and she's in a spot like that?"

But Furia wasn't listening. "Look at my hands!"

The trim little hands were stippled with soot. The spidery black hairs on their narrow backs had been singed off by the brush fire.

"I'm sorry about that," Malone said. In that TV drama he had seen recently, where the escaped convicts took over a suburban household led by a kill-crazy nut, the father had defied the criminals and talked tough to them through the whole thing. He had thought the father nuttier than the convicts. You don't get tough with a desperate criminal holding a gun on you, not if you want you and yours to keep on living. "My wife has some ointment if you got a burn."

"Shove it! Where's the kid?"

Malone half rose. Ellen was standing there like a deer.

He saw her throat move as she swallowed. "What are you going to do to her?"

"That's for me to know and you to find out, missus! Give me the bag."

Malone got all the way up, taking it slow, as he had done approaching the bobcat. He had no idea what he was about. I'll have to do something, I can't just let him shoot us down without lifting a finger. My bare hands against two guns ... Ellen ... Bibby ... Maybe if I talk. The way I say it.

"Look, Mr. Furia," Malone said.

68

"The bag!"

"I'm trying to tell you. I got home with my daughter tonight to find my wife practically in hysterics. This afternoon, while she had to go to the bathroom, somebody got into the house and ran off with the money. No, I swear to God! We knew how sore you'd be, and we've been sitting here trying to figure out—"

An ammunition dump exploded. When the peace fell Malone found himself sitting on the floor with his back against the sofa seat holding his shattered head, Ellen moaning and batting his hand away and dabbing at the wound with a bloody handkerchief, Furia an arm's length away, the Colt in his fist shaking. Malone had not even seen the barrel coming.

He shook his head cautiously, trying to clear it.

"He's lying," the blonde woman said. "Don't you believe him, Fure."

"Heisting us," Hinch snarled. "Let me at the sonofabitch, Fure. I'll open him up."

"I'm handling this!" Furia shouted. He poised the pistol over Malone's head. "You want another clout, smart cop? Or I should put a bullet in your old lady's ear? Now you tell me and you tell it like it is. Where's that bag?"

Malone raised his arm defensively. There was a rising howl in his head that overrode argument and any sort of rational plan. All he could think of was I'm going to get my brains splashed over my own rug by my own gun in front of my own wife without a lousy prayer to help her or Bibby or myself and then they'll get it, too.

"He's telling you the truth, Mr. Furia," Ellen screeched. "It was stolen from me by some man with a stocking over his head. I came out of the bathroom and he hit me over the head with my St. Francis, the pieces are in the garbage pail if you don't believe me. Look at the lump on my head if you don't believe me."

Furia seized her by the hair and yanked her backward. Malone to his own surprise made a feeble attempt to get at him. Furia kicked him in the jaw. Everything stopped.

When it started again Furia was saying in a worried way, "I don't get it."

"So she's got a lump," the woman Goldie said. "How do we know she got it like she says?"

"Yeah," Hinch said. "She could of fell down or something."

"But you saw the pieces of that statue in the pail," Furia said.

"So what?" Goldie said. "She broke it herself to make it look good, Fure. That's the way I see it."

"The gall," Hinch said. "To heist us out of our own heist!"

"They're lying all right, Fure."

"You're lying!" Furia yelped.

"You know we're not," Malone heard Ellen cry. He wanted to stop whatever she was going to say, push Ellen to the wall and thinking is out. But he had no strength to do anything. I wonder if he broke my jaw. "You're putting on a great big act for your two friends!" Ellen cried. "You came here today and stole that bag so you could keep all the money for yourself."

"Me?" Furia screamed.

Malone thought Furia was going to throw a fit on the carpet. The prospect turned him on. The howling cut off, the dark began to turn gray. He pulled himself back to a sitting position. He could feel the restorative adrenaline shooting. He'll turn on Ellen now. Malone bunched himself.

But it was a funny thing how Furia calmed down. He did not throw a fit. He did not turn on Ellen. He made no further move toward Malone. Instead he backed off with the Colt half raised, and when he spoke it was to Hinch and the blonde, in a wary tone. Malone saw his trigger finger tighten the least bit.

"You fall for that, Hinch?"

Hinch was staring at him. "You could of, Fure," he said. "While me and Goldie was in town."

"I never left the shack!"

"Fure wouldn't do a thing like that," Goldie said to Hinch. "Not Fure. Aren't you the clever one?" she said to Ellen. "Trying to split us up."

"She's trying to split us up," Furia said. "Yeah. She figures she can get us in a three-way fight they might find a chance to cut out. You see that, Hinch?"

Hinch hesitated. "I guess," he said.

"You better believe it." He turned to the Malones, gesturing with the revolver. "Sit down!"

Malone pulled himself up to the sofa. Ellen fell down beside him.

"Now," Furia said. "Payup time, folks. Where's that twenty-four grand?"

"Do you think I'd pull a stunt like this and put my family in danger of getting shot?" Malone said. He sensed a hairline advantage, a sliver of crack in the doom. He tried to keep the thump and throb of his head and jaw out of his voice, you don't show weakness to an animal. "Just to get somebody's payroll back because I'm a cop? Or even to keep it for myself? You can beat up on us, torture us, kill us, we can't tell you what we don't know. We're telling the truth. Somebody sneaked in here today and half brained my wife and took the bag. She didn't even get a good look at him."

Furia pounced. "Then why'd she say it was me? Huh? Huh?"

"Because nobody knew the money was here except us and you three. We didn't take it, so we figured it had to be one of you. As my wife was falling she saw he wasn't a big man. If he wasn't a big man we didn't see how it could be anybody but you. Anyway, that's what we figured. Maybe we were wrong, Mr. Furia. Maybe it was some housebreaker who just happened to pick our place today to see what he could steal and hit the jackpot. But that's the way it happened. That's all we know."

The eyes in the mask blinked uncertainly.

"He's a real con, this cop," Goldie said. "A regular mouthpiece. You going to swallow this, Fure?"

"See?" Hinch said. "He says it couldn't of been me."

"No," Furia said. "No, I ain't, Goldie! It's a stall, all right. You and Hinch turn this dump upside down. After we find our dough I'll learn this smartmouth who he's dealing with."

The first search was slapdash. Malone saw half a dozen places in the parlor where the money could have been hidden that Hinch missed. And from the sounds of Goldie's hunt upstairs, the rapidity with which she went through the bedrooms told the same story. The Malones sat with clasped hands under Furia's gun, straining for the first whimper of Barbara overhead, but she slept through the noise.

At one point in the dream Ellen asked if she could go get ice for her husband's jaw and something for his head, but Furia sneered, "You're breaking my heart," and Malone had to lick the blood off his lips. It was still trickling down from his hair.

Hinch was crashing around in the cellar when Goldie

came downstairs lugging Malone's rifle and the boxes of ammunition.

"Look what I found, Fure."

She offered it to him like a mother with candy. He grabbed it with a snarl of pleasure. But he had regressed, it was not the sweet thing he wanted, and he flung it back at her.

"A lousy .22! No dough?"

"I couldn't find it."

Furia ran over to the landing under the stairs and yelled down, "Any sign of it, Hinch?" and when Hinch came clumping up shaking his head Furia ran back and jabbed Malone's throat with the Colt and squealed, "Where is it, you mother lover?" while Ellen, eyes starting from her head, tried to cover him with her body and to Malone's surprise the woman Goldie took hold of Furia's arm with her free hand and pulled him off.

"Shooting them now won't get us our money, Fure. Fure, you listening to me? What good are they dead?" which sounded true to Malone and left him feeling gratitude, that was the New England tradition talking, her good old Yankee horse sense. Bless you, Goldie Whoever-you-are.

Furia tore the mask from his face and for the first time Malone and his wife saw him in the flesh, a corpse-face with the shine of corruption and ears like the White Rabbit's in Barbara's tattered *Alice* and the sad dead expression of a younger version of the little comic on the Smothers Brothers show, Pat Paulsen, but without the humanity or discipline, one of life's rejects, as frightening as an incurable disease.

He seemed to need air.

"You okay, Fure?" Goldie asked. She sounded concerned.

Furia batted her hand away and dropped into the rocker breathing like a fish. He kept hugging the revolver. Hinch and the automatic were holding up the arch looking at Furia with anxiety and a little something extra. A doubt?

Malone shut his eyes.

When he opened them Goldie was saying, "Why not, Fure? We can hole in here for a day or even two and like really take the place apart. That money's here, it's got to be. Right?"

She had taken her mask off, too. Her hair was just-

72

polished brass. The mask had smeared her makeup, it gave her features a blurred look like the TV sometimes when it pulsed. Malone squinted, trying again to place her, but she kept just out of reach. She was younger and must have been fresher then, not runny around the edges, maybe that's why I can't put my finger on it.

He stopped trying because Ellen was leaning her head on his shoulder and her face was turned up, her eyes were faraway glass. Even if we get out of this she'll never be the same, she'll have nightmares the rest of her life, she'll make a nervous wreck out of Bibby, she won't let the kid out of her sight ... and never, never forgive me. Not because all this is my fault but because I somehow didn't rise to it like one of her heroes, Sean Connery, Peter O'Toole, Michael Caine, or her special favorite Spencer Tracy on the Late Late Show the two or three nights a month when the cramps keep her from sleeping. I'm the dropout of her dreams, a smalltown hick who can't make it even medium-sized. And the cop tag a big gas.

Malone hauled himself back to what was going on. Furia had recovered, he was the boss man again. "Didn't you hear what I said, fuzz? You pay attention when I speak!"

"I'm sorry," Malone said. "What did you say? My head aches."

"I said we're moving in on you till we find that bread. You got nosy neighbors?"

"No," Malone said.

"How about delivery men?"

"Just milk. He leaves it on the porch around eight A.M."

"The rube who delivers the mail."

"He drops it in our mailbox near the gate."

"That's all?"

Malone nodded with caution. His head felt like a bongo drum.

"Well, just in case. Anybody comes to the door and asks, we're relatives from out of town. How'd you like me for a relative, missus?"

Ellen almost said something.

"Not good enough for you, ha?"

"I didn't say that," Ellen said.

Furia laughed. "You got it, fuzz?"

"Yes," Malone said.

"You, too, missus?"

73

Ellen gulped something and finally nodded.

"And don't let me catch you trying to use the phone, I'll break your dainty ladyfingers one at a time or, hell, why not? I'll sick Hinch onto you. You like that, Hinch?"

"Mama mia," Hinch said. "What I could do with her."

Malone was hit by ice water. I never thought of that. I never thought of that danger to Ellen.

"Now Hinch," Furia said. "This is a nice lady. Don't go thinking none of your dirty thoughts about Mrs. Fuzz." Goodhumored now, the thing was settled for him by Goldie and he can act the big brass with the reverse of responsibility—ordering the tactics after the chain-of-command below works out the strategy, a hell of a way to run a war. But it was a cockeyed war. Malone kept his eyes on Hinch.

Hinch took off his bear mask, too. No doubt to give Ellen the benefit of his manly beauty. He was looking pleased. Malone's glimpse of that Neanderthal face in the clearing had hardly prepared him for the reality of the closeup. He could imagine how Ellen was feeling at her first look, especially with thoughts of rape trembling in her head. He felt her shudder and he wanted to tell her that gorillas were peaceable animals, it was the sort of thing he would have said to Barbara to hush a fear. But Ellen shuddered again and burrowed closer, a big smart girl who knew the difference between a fairy tale and seeing it like it is, baby. Malone found himself fumbling around with a prayer.

"That goes for both of you," Furia said. "If the phone rings you don't answer without me or Goldie listening in. And about the door, front or back. Anybody comes you don't open till I give you the nod. Got all that?"

Malone said they did. Ellen said nothing.

"Okay. Soon as we tear your bedroom apart I'll let the two of you go up there, I'm sick of looking at you. But you stay there and no tricks. Remember about that phone."

"There's no phone in their bedroom," Goldie said.

"Anywhere."

"My child," Ellen said. "Is it all right if we take my child in with us?" She added quickly, "In case she wakes up, Mr. Furia. I don't want her to be any trouble to you."

"After we search your room, okay." Her humility seemed to gentle him. Or maybe he's turned on. Can he be

74

high on junk or LSD? No, not him. He's got to have control.

"She can remind you the spot you're in, missus."

Malone saw suddenly that Furia's bag was fear.

"Thank you," Ellen said humbly.

Furia had done a job on their room all right. While Hinch held the Walther on them downstairs. Every once in a while making a face at Ellen. He seemed to enjoy watching her shrivel and blanch. Malone could see Hinch's lips, red and wet as fresh blood, and occasionally the gray tip of his tongue. Those lips on Ellen. The picture made him pull his legs up as if he had been kicked in the groin.

Everything in their bureau drawers had been tossed every which way. The clothes in their closet had been ripped apart garment by garment. The bedroom rug, a handhooked American Colonial that Ellen had wheedled out of her mother, had been slashed in three places—how could it have hidden anything?—and kicked aside. A loose board of the old chestnut floor Ellen kept in a perpetual gleam had been hacked with Malone's handax from the cellar and pried up; they could see in the cavity before Malone replaced it a fossilized rat's nest that had probably been there for generations. Their imitation maple double bed had been taken apart and two of the slats broken, sleep-on-that-damn-you they seemed to say in Furia's alto, Malone had had to put the bed together again before they could transfer Bibby from her room. The child's head was lying on his hunting jacket. Furia's switchblade had disemboweled their two pillows, goose feathers lay all over the room.

They sat on the floor at the foot of the bed in the wreckage listening to Barbara's heavy breathing. She had waked from her alcoholic sleep when Malone picked her up and begun to cry, complaining that her head hurt, and Ellen had had to get the boss man's permission to go for an aspirin in the upstairs bathroom. She finally got Bibby back to sleep. Malone was holding an icebag to his swollen jaw, and with the bandage on his bloody head that Ellen had applied he looked like a refugee from a defeated army.

Ellen said with a shiver, "Hold me, Loney."

He held her.

"I'm scared."

"We're still alive," Malone said.

The Irish in her stirred, and she showed the faintest dimple. "You call this living?"

He lowered the icebag to kiss her. "That's my girl."

"Loney, are we going to get out of this?"

"I think we're all right for the time being."

"And how long is that?"

He was silent.

"Couldn't you make a rope out of the bedclothes and climb out the window while they're tearing up the house?" She's back at the movies again. "You could make a call to Chief Secco from the Cunninghams' or the Rochelles' . . ."

"How long do you think you and Bibby would last if they found me gone? You've got to face it, Ellen. We're in this alone."

She was silent.

I'm in this alone.

A glass crashed downstairs and they heard Hinch laughing. He's found the bottle of scotch Don James gave me for finally catching that white kid who kept heaving trashcans through their front windows. He tried not to think of Hinch drunk and tightened his grip on Ellen.

After a while Malone said, "Our best chance is if we can get the money back or at least figure out who took it. I could maybe make a deal with Furia, the money for him letting us go."

"I thought you thought Furia stole it."

"I thought he did. Now I'm not sure. A punk like him could put on an act, I suppose, but I think I'd see through it, I can usually tell when they're lying. He sounded pretty convincing to me."

"But if it wasn't Furia who could it have been? Maybe it was Hinch after all, Loney. He could have been like in a crouch—"

"Can't you remember anything else about the man who hit you?"

She set her head back against the patchwork quilt. "I told you all I saw."

"Sometimes things can come back. We've got to try, baby. Ellen?"

"Yes?"

"I know you're fagged out, but don't go to sleep on me now. Think! His suit. What color was it?"

Ellen's head rolled a negative.

"Was it a suit? Or could it have been a sports outfit?

76

Did the pants and jacket match?"

"I don't know. I didn't notice."

"Or maybe a leather jacket?"

She shook her head again.

"Could he have been wearing a topcoat?"

"I just didn't see, Loney."

"A hat?"

"No," Ellen said this time. "No hat, or I'd remember. The stocking was drawn over his whole head."

"You can see *something* of the face through one of those sheer stockings. Do you remember anything about his face?"

"Just a mashed nose."

"Mashed? Like Hinch's?"

"A stocking would mash . . . anybody's . . . nose . . ."

"Ellen, you're falling asleep again." He shook her, and she opened her eyes.

"I'm sorry."

"Hair? Ears? Tie? Hands? Feet?"

She kept shaking her head. But then her eyes got big and she pushed away from the bed. "His feet, Loney! He was wearing galoshes. Or overshoes."

"Overshoes." Malone stared at her. "Today? It's been dry all day, not a cloud in the sky. You sure, Ellen?"

She nodded.

"That's a hot one. Overshoes . . . What's the matter?"

"I just remembered something else."

"What?"

"His hands. He was wearing gloves. I saw the hand coming down after I was hit. I didn't see flesh. It was a man's glove. Black leather."

"Gloves," Malone muttered. "That could figure. If he kept his face covered he might also be careful not to leave his fingerprints around . . . if he was, say, a housebreaker."

"In New Bradford?" Ellen actually smiled. "You're making like a detective again, Officer. Why would a sneakthief in this town worry about fingerprints?"

"I admit it's a lot likelier one of them, the way we've been figuring. But why gloves? All three of them came here tonight barehanded . . ."

Malone looked surprised at the destination of his train of thought. He set the icebag on the floor carefully and slipped off his shoes and put his fingers to his lips and got up, not like an exhausted man now. He went to the door

77

and listened. When he came back he got down on one knee and said in a whisper, "Ellen, you've kept telling me it was a man hit you. Why a man?"

"Huh?"

"Why've you been saying the one who hit you was a man?"

Ellen frowned. "I don't know. His jacket, the pants—"

"That doesn't make a man. Not these days. These days you can hardly tell some women and men apart. A woman can put on a pair of slacks and a man-style jacket and with her hair squashed down by that tight stocking you wouldn't be able to tell, not from the front and while you were falling from a hit on the head. But there's two things about a woman would be a dead giveaway if they weren't disguised some way and that's her hands and feet!

"That's why she wore the men's overshoes on a dry day and men's gloves. She was taking out insurance in case she was spotted. Remember Hinch saying downstairs he and this Goldie went into town today? Ellen, it's Goldie who's doublecrossing the other two. She must have given Hinch the slip in town and come here on her own.

"She's the one knocked you out. She lifted the bag, and it's a cinch she hid it somewhere before she went back to the cabin. It adds up, because she's been trying like mad to sell Furia that we stole it. Yes, sir. That's it!"

Malone was feeling the small triumph. He craved Ellen's adoration. He wanted her to say, You've redeemed yourself in my eyes, my darling, you're my very own hero, you sure can overcome, I feel safe again.

But all Ellen said was, "All right, Loney, she's got it. How does that help us?"

And of course she's right.

Malone got back up and began to pad about. "That's the problem. What else have we got to work on? Nothing. So we've got to make use of it some way. How?"

"That is the question," Ellen said. She did not sound anything but beat. Her head sank back against the end of the bed.

But Malone's second wind continued to blow. It was something. It was a light where everything before had been black as the inside of the old gravity well out back that hadn't been used in fifty years and was full of green slime, like Furia must be.

"Maybe if we accuse her of it in front of the other two," Ellen murmured.

78

"No, that wouldn't work. She's smart, she's got Furia around her little finger, he'll believe anything she says. She mustn't even suspect we suspect her, Ellen, or she might get Furia to knock us off. I wouldn't put it past her. Deep down she's worse than he is."

"Could we make a deal with her ... ?"

"What have we got to offer? That we'll tell Furia? Even if it put a doubt in his mind we can't prove it to him, and she'd talk him out of it. Up to now, Ellen, she's held him back. She wouldn't hold him back any more." Malone looked down at her. "The way it shapes up, we'll have to somehow find out or figure out where she's hiding it."

"You do that."

"Ellen, we can't give up."

"Who's giving up?"

"You are!"

"What do you want me to do, Loney? I can't fight them with my bare hands." That was it. That was it. "All I know is, I've got my child's life to protect—"

"*We've* got!"

"Do you want them to hear us fighting?"

Malone cracked his knuckles and began padding again.

Ellen's eyelids came down.

"I'm not sleeping," she said. "The light hurts my eyes."

He flipped the switch savagely. But then he collapsed against the wall. This is no good. We're at each other's throats. What did I expect from her? Up against the first real spot in my life and I try to lean on her like I never leaned on even my own mother. She wants to lean on *me*. She's got a right, I'm her husband. It's one man one vote time. You go into the booth and you're all by yourself. The American way.

He buckled down to it like Robinson Crusoe.

"Ellen." Malone shook her gently.

It was much later.

"Loney?" She had fallen asleep. She sat up and groped for his hand. "Is something—did they—?"

"No, they're quiet, they've given up for the night." Malone squatted beside her in the dark. "I've got to talk to you."

"Oh."

"No, this is different. I've been going over the whole thing in my head. I think I'm onto something."

79

"Oh?"

"Ellen, wake up, this could be important. Then you can climb into bed with Bibby. Are you awake?"

"Yes."

"Something struck me funny. How come these creeps picked our house Wednesday night?"

She moved and the floor creaked. "They were running away. Maybe they saw our light on. I don't think anybody else on the block had their lights on when I got back from the movies."

"But why pick Old Bradford Road in the first place? There's a Dead End sign at the entrance off Lovers Hill. A blind man can see it. Robbers running away aren't going to box themselves in on a dead-end street. And another thing. Before I got home from the station Wednesday night, did you tell them I was a cop?"

"Of course not. I was afraid if they knew they might shoot you down as you came in the door."

"Right. But just the same they knew, didn't they? Furia called me a cop straight out. How did he know? I wasn't in uniform. How did he know, Ellen?"

"That is funny."

"I'll tell you how. They had advance information!"

"You mean they saw you on duty in town during the day?"

"Then why did Furia say, 'Freeze, cop,' as soon as I stepped into the house? He couldn't even see my face, they had all the lights out except on the porch, and my back was to that. No, Ellen, they knew without ever having seen me before."

"But how could they?"

"Nanette."

Ellen said, "My God. The girl I've trusted Bibby to all these years! Nanette's in on this, Loney?"

"I don't know. It wouldn't have to be. Remember how many times Nanette's mentioned her older sister, how their parents practically disowned her because she went bad? Ellen, this Goldie is Nanette's sister."

"That's just a guess."

"It's a fact. I knew right away I'd seen her before, years ago, I was sure she came from New Bradford, but I didn't place her till I started asking myself all these questions and then it came to me just like that. Nanette said herself they've kept up a correspondence on the sly since Goldie left home. My guess is Nanette mentioned her regular baby-sitting job for us, and Goldie remembered it when they were in a jam Wednesday night and talked Furia into coming here and taking Bibby as security for the money. So I've got to get to Nanette first thing in the morning—"

"They won't let you go."

"I've got an idea about that, too. Ellen, it's our only lead. I can't pass it up."

"Lead to what? How can it possibly help us?"

Malone got to his feet. "Maybe it can't. But it's better than sitting here like three chickens waiting to get our necks chopped off."

"Oh, Loney, if you only could!"

And that was better, lots better.

He stooped to kiss her. "Now you're getting into that bed, young lady."

"Not unless you do."

"I'll come to bed in a while."

He waited until Ellen's breathing told him she was asleep.

Then he felt around in the dark until he located the loose board. He split a fingernail prying it up and he stretched out on the floor in front of the door with the board in his arms.

I'll have to pull it off in the morning.

Some way.

Friday

The Bottom

His eyes opened to cloudy darkness. The sun rose at a little past six thirty this time of year and so it must be after six. Yes, there goes old man Tyrell's rooster. The cock was past his prime in everything but his doodledooing, he was worse than an alarm clock. The Tyrells were down to one ancient biddy still trying for fertile eggs. Somebody ought to tell the poor old slobs, all four of them, the facts of life.

Eggs.

How do you walk on them?

Malone sat up swallowing a groan and shivering, the house was cold and he had slept without a cover. He stretched and a minefield of muscles went off. When was the last time I sacked out on a bed?

On eggs. How do you walk on them?

He listened. Ellen and Barbara were breathing as if it were an ordinary day. There was a great quiet in the house. So the Three Bears were asleep, too.

He wondered where.

Malone went through his isometric exercises to get the circulation going and when he was satisfied he got to his feet with no noise, which was his objective for more reasons than Ellen and Barbara.

He felt around with his big toe and located the hole and slipped the floorboard back over the rat's nest, thanking the Lord he hadn't had to use it. Hinch must be sleeping off the one he tied on with Don's scotch.

I could get away from them now, maybe all three of us could.

The thought came to Malone with the unexpectedness of all good things, in a rush of warmth.

All we have to do is slip out of the house and down the Hill to the station and we're safe in John's hands and that's the end of the nightmare!

It could be that easy.

Or could it?

He took two minutes to open the bedroom door.

His eyes were used to the half dark now and in his stockinged feet he made his way inches at a time along the hall, hugging the wall so the floor would not creak.

When he came to Barbara's room he found the door shut. With care Malone grasped and turned the porcelain knob and with more care pushed. The door refused to give. *It can't be Furia or Hinch, it must be the woman. But why should she lock the door? If she'd jumped into the hay with Furia I'd have heard them through the wall. It must be Hinch, she doesn't trust Hinch.*

He tucked that thought away with the others he was accumulating.

The door to the spare bedroom across the hall was half open. *Were the two hoods bedded down there?* Malone was puzzled. With his broken nose and a bellyful of scotch, Hinch ought to be sounding off like a freight train.

Malone crossed the hall in a tiptoe stride and pulled up at the other side, holding his breath. He listened some more. Very carefully he looked in, he could see well enough by now. But the room was empty.

One of the cots was gone.

They're sleeping downstairs.

He catfooted to the landing and risked a look over the railing. He could see down into the parlor and he could see through the archway into the entrance hall. The sofa was gone from its place, they had dragged it into the hall and set it up against the front door. A small figure lay curled like a cat on the sofa, covered by Ellen's afghan.

The sight of Furia defenseless tightened Malone's hand

85

and the railing squealed. Furia woke up like a cat, too. The Colt Trooper looked enormous in his hand. Malone dodged back to the protection of the wall, holding his breath.

After a while he heard Furia settle back to sleep.

Hinch must be bedded down in the kitchen on the cot from the spare room, blocking the back door as Furia was blocking the front. Malone strained and heard snores. He's there, all right. Maybe he drank so much that I could ... But there was Furia, who slept like a cat and woke up like one.

Malone made his way back to Ellen and Barbara. In the bedroom he made a slight noise and Ellen shot up in bed.

"Loney?"

The terror in her voice touched him like a live wire. He went over to the bed and stroked her tumbled hair and whispered, "It's all right, honey. Go back to sleep now," and she sighed and did.

Later, at the window, he even considered Ellen's suggestion about a rope of bedclothes. But Ellen and Bibby couldn't climb out without lots of noise and then there'd be hell to pay.

I'll have to play it like it is.

Malone settled down, going over desperately what he had muddled through during the night. Does it stand up? Or is this another pipe dream?

Goldie wouldn't have hidden the payroll where there's any chance Furia might find it. So the cabin is out. Ditto the Chrysler. And she couldn't hide all those bills on her body.

Then where?

Had she set up a place in advance, the way they set up their hideout at Balsam Lake? But she couldn't have known they were going to be hung up in New Bradford because of Pickney finding Tom Howland's body so soon and the roadblocks being set up so fast. Or even if she figured on that, the thing just didn't smell of a planned doublecross before the murder and robbery. The stocking on her head, the men's overshoes and gloves, she must have bought them in town yesterday afternoon when she and Hinch came in, at some store where she could be sure she wasn't known, maybe the Army-Navy Store on Freight Street, Joe Barron was only in New Bradford two years, it all smacked of spur-of-the-moment.

If that was true, then her hiding place for the money must have been picked on the spur of the moment, too.

All right. She's got this loot. And she's smart. She has to choose a hiding place where Furia can't possibly put his hands on it even by accident. Even if he suspects her and tries to muscle it out of her. Even if he makes her tell him. That would be Goldie's style.

All right.

The way it worked out, nobody in town knows the Aztec job was pulled by a gang including a woman. Nobody but Ellen and Bibby and me, and we don't count. That's the way she'd figure. So she can come and go in town like she did yesterday, with just the small risk that she might run into somebody who'd recognize her from the old days. And even if they did, so what? She's back to visit her family. Nothing to tie her in to the crime.

Yes, one likely place. Just the hiding place a smart cookie like Goldie would hit on. I've got to check it out.

But the way things are, where do I go from there?

At this point Malone shut his mind down.

One thing at a time.

He waited with his ear against the door and heard the woman go downstairs and the whistle of the kettle in the kitchen and the spin of Furia's voice.

Ellen was explaining things to Barbara.

"I knew those people were bad," Barbara said in her grownup voice, the one she used when she disapproved of something. "Did Daddy get me back?"

"Yes, darling. How's your head?"

"It feels icky. You know what they did, Mommy? That lady made me drink some *liquor*. She said it would make me sleep. I didn't want to, it tasted awful, but she forced me."

"I know, baby. Don't think about it."

"Why did I sleep in your bed last night?"

"They're here in the house, Bibby," Malone said. "I want you and your mother to stay in this room. Be very quiet and do what Mommy says."

"Where are you going, Daddy?"

"I may have to go out for a while."

"I don't want you to."

"Now none of that," Malone said. He turned away.

"I'm *famished*." It was her latest favorite word.

"I'll get you some breakfast later," Ellen said.

"Ellen, I'm going down," Malone said.

"Loney, for God's sake."

"Don't worry. Just stay up here unless they call you. Do exactly what they say. Don't cross them."

"What are you going to do?"

"Try to get Furia to let me go into town."

"Do you think he will?"

"He's got you and Bibby."

"How long will you be gone?"

"I don't know. I'll be back as soon as I can."

Malone opened the door. He could hear Hinch grousing and Goldie's sarcastic laugh. He went over and kissed Barbara and then Ellen and left in a hurry so that he would not have to see their faces any more.

They were in the kitchen slurping coffee. The kitchen looked like a battlefield on the morning after. They had yanked out every drawer and emptied every cupboard. Dishes and cutlery and pots and bottles and boxes of cereal lay strewn about like the unburied dead. The door to the freezer compartment was open and Malone saw that half Ellen's supply of meat was gone.

"Well look who's here," Goldie said. It seemed to him her brightness was forced. She's walking on eggs, too.

"Who told you to come down, fuzz?" Hinch growled. He had a growth of red pig bristles and his eyes were shot with pig pink.

"Shut up, Hinch." Furia looked at Malone over his cup. "Going somewheres?" Malone had changed into his good civvy suit. He was wearing a tie.

"I'd like to talk to you."

"Now that's being a smart fuzz."

"I mean about—"

"I thought you're ready to talk."

"Sure," Malone said. "I'll tell you everything I can, Mr. Furia. But what I mean—"

"For openers, how about where you stashed my loot?"

"I told you, I didn't take it. For one thing I had no time."

He tried to keep his eyes off the revolver on the table beside Furia's cup. Hinch had the rifle and the automatic.

"Okay, you had no time. But your missus did. Where did she hide it?"

"She didn't take it either. I don't know what I can do, Mr. Furia, but keep telling you that. Ellen's not out of her

88

mind, you had our daughter. Look, I know this town inside out. If some local Lightfinger Louie snatched that bag yesterday, which is what I think happened, I could maybe get a line on him. If you'll let me nose around. I want you to get the money and get out of here as bad as you do, Mr. Furia."

"It's a trick," Hinch complained. "Don't listen to him, Fure. I don't know why you won't let me bang it out of him."

"Because he just ain't the bang-out type," Furia said. "Drink your coffee, Hinch. You think it's a trick, too, Goldie?"

Goldie shrugged in a swirl of hair. She had not bothered to brush it and she looked like a witch. "I still say they took it. He's stalling for time."

"I don't know." Furia pulled on his longish nose. Then he drummed on the table. He had scrubbed the soot off his hands and they were clean and neat again. "Suppose they see you?"

"Who?" Malone said.

"The fuzz. Your buddies. I was going to tell you to call in sick."

"That isn't necessary," Malone said quickly. "The flu hit the department and I did double tricks for four days running. The Chief gave me a couple days off to rest up. So nobody'll think anything of it if I'm seen in town in civvies."

"He's telling the truth about that, anyways," Furia said. "I read in this New Bradford paper yesterday about how the flu hit the cops."

Goldie said, "I still don't like it."

"Who asked you?"

"You did."

"Well, I'm letting him go in. He ain't going to be a hero, not with his wife and kid with us. Wait a second, fuzz." Furia picked up the revolver. "Go upstairs, Goldie, and make sure those two are okay."

Goldie pushed away from the table and brushed past Malone without a glance. She's walking on eggs is right. He stood where he was respectfully.

"Okay," Goldie called down.

"Okay," Furia said. "Your story is this was an outside heist, Malone, you prove it. You got till one o'clock. You either bring me that bread or proof where it is or who's

89

got it. If you know what's good for the missus and kid upstairs. Oh, and one more thing."

"Yes?" Malone said.

"When you come back here you better not have nobody with you. And don't try any hairy stunts like coming back heeled. Put it out of your clyde. Because you do that and Hinch and me we're going to have to decorate your floor with your wife and kid's brains. Kapeesh?"

"I kapeesh."

The Vorsheks lived in the Hollow near a narrow bend in the Tonekeneke. It was a settlement of poor men's houses huddled in the companionship of misery, but with an impersonal beauty unknown to city slums. The usual dirty children played on the tincan landscape or on the lunar stones of the riverbed during droughts and there were always flapping lines of wash, but backyards in the spring showed unbuyable stands of very old magnolias in impossible bloom, and everywhere in the summer vegetable plots as green and true as Japanese gardens.

Peter Vorshek worked in the incubator rooms at Hurley's chicken farm. Mrs. Vorshek did handironing for the ladies of New Bradford to boost the family budget, her free time given passionately to her church. Their daughter Nanette ran a loom at the New Bradford Knitting Mill and baby-sat nights for a few favored clients. The Vorsheks were of Slovak or Czech stock, Malone had never known which. The old man, who carried around with him the smell of chickenshit, still spoke with an accent. He had the European peasant's awe of authority. He always called Malone "Mr. Poleetsman."

Malone pulled the Saab up at the front gate and got out. Nanette was perched in a rocker on the porch reading a movie magazine. She was wearing skintight slacks and a turtleneck.

They look a lot alike all right.

"Mr. Malone." Nanette jumped up. "Something wrong with Bibby? I had to leave early Wednesday night because my mother was sick—she still is, that's why I'm staying home from work—"

"I know, my wife told me," Malone said.

"Oh! What happened to your head and face?"

"A little accident. Mind if I sit down a minute, Nanette?"

"Mind? I should say not."

She sat down looking flattered. He took the other chair and made his onceover casual. She was a large girl, larger than Goldie in every department, with the heavy Vorshek features but plainer than Goldie's, the pug nose, the high bones, the straight brown hair her sister camouflaged. He had seen Nanette at least once a week since her high school days, but he had never absorbed more than an impression of a sort of homely niceness, Bibby worshiped her and she was reliable, which was all he cared about. From what he had heard she rarely went out on a date. The talk among the studs was that she couldn't be made, her old man and old lady kept her on too short a leash, the YPF type, they said, a hardnose churchgoer, as tough to crack as a nun. But Malone thought he saw a certain something in her hazel eyes.

She's wondering why I'm here. No sign of being scared or worried like she'd surely show if she was in on this with Goldie and the two hoods. My hunch was right, she probably doesn't even know her sister is in town.

"My father's working and my mother's in bed," Nanette said with a downward look. For some reason her face was red. "You want to see mom, Mr. Malone?"

"I'm here to see you," Malone said. "I took a chance you'd be home, knowing Mrs. Vorshek is down sick." He managed a smile.

"Mrs. Malone know you're here?" He could barely hear her.

"Yes. Why?"

"Oh, nothing."

By God, she's got a thing for me. All these years and I never knew. He had been racking his brains trying to work out an approach, and he had come up the walk still trying. This could be the break.

"Nanette."

She looked up.

"How long have you known me?"

She giggled. "That's a funny question, Mr. Malone. You know how long. Years."

"Have I ever made a pass at you?"

"You? Oh, no!"

"Ever catch me in a lie, or trying to take advantage of you?"

"I should say not."

"Do you trust me, Nanette?"

"I guess I do. I mean sure."

"I'm glad. Because I'm going to have to trust you, too. In a very important thing. Something I can't even tell you about. I need information."

"From *me*?"

"From Goldie's sister."

She went white. She whispered, "Wait a minute," and jumped up and ran into the house. When she came back she said, "It's okay, mom's sleeping," and pulled the rocker closer to Malone and sat down on the edge and clasped her big hands on her knees. "She's in trouble, isn't she?"

"Yes," Malone said. "But I can't tell you what trouble, Nanette, or anything about it. All I can do is ask you to help me."

Her lips came together. "You want me to do something against my own sister."

"The kind of trouble Goldie's in, Nanette, she can't get out of. Whatever you do or don't do, sooner or later she's going to have to pay for it. Nothing can make it worse for her. But by cooperating you can maybe help Bibby and Mrs. Malone and me. *We're* in trouble through no fault of our own. Bad trouble."

"Because of Goldie?"

He was silent. Then he said, "Will you help us?"

"I don't get it."

"I wish I could tell you, Nanette, I really do. But there are reasons why I can't. Will you help us?"

She banged back in the rocker and began to rock in little fast rocks, like an angry old lady, lips' fleshiness thinned, hairy brows drawn tight. Malone waited patiently.

"It'll hurt Goldie?"

"I told you, it can't hurt her more than she's already hurt herself. You'll just have to take my word for that, Nanette. You've got to make up your mind that your sister made the bed she's lying in. But you can help out people who've always treated you right and never did anything against you."

"She's in New Bradford, isn't she?"

"I didn't say that. I didn't say anything, and I'm not going to. Nanette, look at me."

She looked at him.

"I'm desperate. I mean it."

Whatever she saw in his eyes, it made her stop rocking. She looked out over the porch rail at the hills, seeing something he could not. "I guess I always knew Goldie would wind up bad. When I was a little girl I used to look up to her because she was so much prettier and smarter than me and the boys were all ape over her. And because she wasn't scared of my parents. She'd sass papa back to his face something awful and he'd smack her hard and she'd never even cry, I thought she was so brave ... What do you want, Mr. Malone?"

He let out his breath. "When is the last time you saw her?"

"Years ago."

"You didn't see her, say, this past summer?"

"This year? No."

"Does she ever write to you?"

"Once in a while. Not often, but regular, if you know what I mean. From all kinds of places. My father always goes to work before the mailman comes, but I get to the mailbox in the morning before my mother in case there's a letter from Goldie. Mom would tear it up on the spot if she got there first. My parents are still very Old Country, they never changed. Since Goldie ran away they won't even let me mention her name. Not that she uses it any more, the Vorshek, I mean. She calls herself Goldie Vanderbilt, I don't know why."

Malone heard her out. When she stopped he said casually, "Ever save any of her letters?"

Jesus let this be it.

"Oh, all of them," Nanette said. "I keep them hid in my old toy chest in the attic that mama hasn't touched for years."

"Could I please see her last letter?"

Nanette got up without a word and went into the house. Malone sat on the Vorshek porch looking out at the half-naked willows stooped over the river and the fading hump of hill beyond, seeing nothing but his predicament.

Even if my hunch proves out I'm a long way from home.

One step at a time is how you have to do it.

Then you figure out where you go from there.

Till one o'clock.

At this point Malone's mind got stuck again.

When Nanette came back she was in a hurry. Her red hands were clasped about an envelope, trying to hide it. Malone had never noticed before that her fingernails were bitten all the way down.

"Mama's getting restless," she whispered. "You better go, Mr. Malone, before she wakes up. I don't want to have to explain what you're doing here." She shoved the letter into his hand. "Put it away."

He put it into his pocket without looking at it.

"It isn't typewritten?"

"Goldie don't know how to type."

"Nanette, if I just knew how to thank you."

"Go on, Mr. Malone!"

A hundred yards shy of the turnoff from the Hollow road to The Pike, Malone pulled the Saab over and killed his engine.

The envelope was cheap supermarket stuff but the note-paper was heavy and had a gold *GV* monogram on it and a powerful perfume. The envelope was postmarked JERSEY CITY, N.J. 23 OCT, the return address at the upper left said "G. Vanderbilt, care P.O. General Delivery, Boston, Mass. 02100." The letter was less than a month old, just what the doctor ordered, a recent specimen, God knows I'm no expert, but this ought to do it.

From bitter compulsion he read the letter. It was full of news that couldn't be pinned down: her "job" (without specification—and what sort of job would it be that spanned Jersey City and Boston?—that wasn't very smart, Miss Vanderbilt), her "loaded boy friend" (no name), the glamorous nightspots, the marvelous clothes, the great times, and so on and on, no mention of a Furia or a Hinch or the grimy life the threesome must lead . . . all of it a fairy tale to impress the yokel kid sister (like the elegant stationery) and maybe get her to follow Goldie Vanderbilt's example and split from the old family homestead out of some vicious need to corrupt Nanette and break what was left of the Vorsheks' hearts.

The bitch.

The only good thing was that she wasn't fooling anybody but herself. Maybe Nanette once felt envious, swallowing the fairy tales, but not any more; she knew it was all made up. She probably looked forward to the perfumed letters the way she did to a rerun of *Snow White* or a costume movie in bigger-than-life Panavision.

94

Malone put the letter carefully away, started the Saab, and drove on into town.

He waited on the three-seater leatherette bench outside the steel railing while Wally Bagshott turned down a nervous young couple for a personal loan. Wallace L. Bagshott was president of The Taugus County National Bank, founded by his great-grandfather in the days of the granite quarry and the hitching post. A Bagshott had settled New Bradford; the old Bagshott house, dated 1694, still overlooked the Green, a historic showplace opened to the public one day a year. The double statue on the Green of Zebediah and Zipporah Bagshott, known to the town as the Zizzes, was the favorite privy of the starlings.

"Wes, boy." Bagshott had ushered the young couple out and was smiling over at Malone. "You want to see me?"

Malone jumped up. The banker was tanned halfway up his scalp, a result of spending all his free time hacking divots out of the New Bradford golf course. His employees called him "Smiley" behind his back and his customers "Wally the Knife," on explosive occasions to his face.

"Hey, you look like you're in line for a couple of Purple Hearts. What happened to you?"

"Believe it or not, I fell down the stairs, Wally—"

"What are you doing out of uniform? John fire you I hope I hope? You know my standing offer—"

"I'm off duty," Malone said, going through the gate. "Wally, I have to talk to you."

"Squattee voo." The banker sat down, still smiling. "Though if it's about a personal loan, Wes, I've got to tell you right off—"

"It's not about a loan."

"That's a load off. The way things are we're having to tighten up. Well! Sit down, Wes." Malone sat down. "How's the better half? That's one damn fine piece you grabbed off. Every time Ellen comes in my tellers get all worked up. And not just my tellers if you know what I mean. Ha-ha."

"Look, Wally," Malone said.

"No offense, Wes, no offense. Share the wealth is my motto. Talking about that, terrible thing about Tom Howland, isn't it? They say he was in on it."

"I wouldn't know. Wally, I need a favor."

"Oh?" Bagshott immediately stopped smiling.

"I'd like to inspect your safe deposit records."

"What for?"

"I can't tell you anything about it. Except that it's important."

"Well, I don't know. You're out of uniform—"

"Let's say it's undercover work."

"No kid?" The banker leaned forward eagerly. "It's about this stickup, isn't it?"

Malone was quiet.

"Well, if you can't. Okay, Wes, I don't see why not, seeing you're an officer of the law."

"One thing, Wally. I've got to ask you to keep this absolutely to yourself."

"You know me, pal." Bagshott winked. "Tightest snatch in town."

He waved his Masonic ring and led the way to the rear of the bank. He dismissed the woman on duty in the Safe Deposit Department and unlocked a drawer.

"Here's the check-in card."

"The one they sign when they want to get into their box?"

"Isn't that what you want to see?"

"Yes. But I'm also interested in your latest applications for box rentals."

"How far back you want to go?"

"Yesterday."

The banker looked startled. "Yesterday?"

Malone nodded.

"You mean to say—?"

"I'm not meaning to say anything. Just let me have them, would you mind?"

Bagshott took out three cards. He was so conscious of the hot breath of crime that he broke his own rule about never allowing himself to look worried. "Three new boxes rented yesterday," he said with a careful look around. "They haven't even been put in the master file yet."

"I'd like to take these into one of the rooms."

"Good idea. Sure thing."

"Alone."

Bagshott frowned. Then he walked quickly away.

Malone went into the nearest unoccupied cubicle and shut the door. He sat down at the desk and pulled the light chain and spread the cards and took Goldie's letter from his pocket.

He spotted it at once. "Georgette Valencia, The Cascades, Southville." The Cascades was a twenty-year-old housing development straddling the town line, in an unincorporated village policed on contract by the New Bradford department. Malone knew every family in the Southville district. No one of that name lived there. So the "Georgette Valencia" was a phony.

For confirmation, the Gs and Vs in the signatures on the application and check-in cards were identically formed with those in Goldie's letter, the Gs with a squared-off bottom line instead of the usual curve, the Vs like hasty checkmarks. Even the small ts were the same, with the crossmarks tilted downward from right to left in a fancy swash.

No doubt about it, Georgette Valencia was Goldie Vorshek, alias Goldie Vanderbilt.

So I doped it right. Goldie hijacked the stolen payroll and stashed it in the one place where nobody else could get to it, a safe deposit box in the bank.

So now I've got the money back.

Well, not exactly got it back, but I know where I can lay my hands on it.

Not exactly lay my hands on it, unless . . .

Malone stowed the letter away, gathered up the cards, turned off the light and went out into the banking room. Bagshott was alone at his desk, talking on the phone. The moment he saw Malone he hung up. Malone laid the cards on the desk and said, "I'd like to get into one of your boxes."

The banker looked around. "Sure, Wes," he said. "Sit down, make it look natural. I mean sure, soon as you bring me the court order."

Malone lowered himself into the chair, holding onto the corner of Bagshott's desk. "You won't let me see it without the judge's authorization?"

"I can't, Wes. You know the law."

"Well, how about these cards? If I could just borrow them for a few hours—"

Bagshott stared. It was his banker's stare, the fish eye. "There's something funny about this. You trying to pull something, Wes? You know I can't let any official records out of the bank. What's going on?"

"I can't tell you."

"Which box is it?"

Malone got up and walked out.

He drove over to Elwood's and sank onto a stool. The breakfast rush was over and the diner was almost empty. He was grateful that no one had the juke box going. His head was kicking up a storm.

He was famished. He had not been conscious of his hunger until this moment. I haven't eaten in how long is it?

"Morning, morning, Wes," Elwood said, slapping his rag around. "Some excitement."

"I can live without it, Ave," Malone said. "Double o.j., wheats and sausage, stack of toast, coffee."

"You sound starved," the old man cracked. "Like it's your last meal."

Malone tried to appreciate the joke.

"And peaked, too. Damn shame how they run you boys ragged." Elwood went into his kitchen wagging his head.

Run ragged.

That's for sure, Ave.

What do I do now?

I can't go to the judge without telling him why I want the order, and if I do that I set Ellen and Bibby up for cemetery plots. Judge Trudeau is a stickler for the law books, people don't mean a goddam to him, he'd have the house surrounded by state police in ten minutes. So I can't get into the box. I can't produce the money for Furia.

I can't even take possession of the bank forms that along with Goldie's letter would show Furia she rented the safe deposit box. And without proof that she doublecrossed him he wouldn't believe me, it would be my word against hers, and I don't go to bed with him. He'd get so worked up about what he'd think was a stall he'd likely shoot the three of us on the spot.

So where do we go from here.

Nowhere.

End of the line.

There's just so much a man can do by himself.

It came to Malone suddenly that he had just thought a profound thought. It was the exact story of his life.

Ellen didn't start calling me The Malone Ranger just for laughs. She tagged me good from the start. Wes Malone against the world and to hell with you, neighbor. Malone the on-his-own-two-feet guy, he asks nothing from nobody. Not even from the only man in the world he respects and trusts. Too proud, that's Loney. Maybe too sore at the whole raw deal that began with the old man

98

crawling into the sack every night giving nothing to anyone, not so much as a word or a look, and the mother cursing her life and taking with both tobacco-stained hands. So you grow up giving in spite of yourself.

Giving is giving out.

Taking is giving in.

Giving-out keeps you on top of the enemy.

Giving-in is crawling on your belly to the sonofabitch world.

Or is it? Is it being a loser to ask for a helping hand when you can't make it any more on your own? What the hell else is the Marine buddy system but I'm-right-here-brother?

That's why I was a lousy grunt.

That's why I'm a lousy cop and husband and father. That's why John and Ellen look at me the way they do sometimes, Bibby's too young to know better.

I've been kidding myself. And shortchanging them.

But there's the but.

Can I do it?

My whole life says no.

My whole life is my bag, that's been my hangup. Now I've got to. No choices left. My back to the wall and Ellen's and Bibby's, too.

Their whole lives are on the line.

That's what it comes down to.

Malone looked up at the diner clock.

Ten minutes past eleven.

Less than two hours to putup time.

He dropped a couple of one-dollar bills on the counter not bothering to wait for change I might chicken. And ran.

John Secco got up and took a few turns. He hated his private office and spent as little time as possible in it. It was down the hall from the three cells and it was not much bigger than they were, whitewashed brick walls and nothing on them, the only real difference was a door instead of bars. He looked tired, almost as tired as Malone.

Malone watched him.

After the third turn Malone said stiffly, "If you want my badge, John."

The chief stopped. He had black brows under the gray

99

thatch and they went up like windowshades. "What are you talking about?"

"I know I ought to have come to you right off. Any way I slice it I'm an officer of the law—"

"Any way you slice it you're Ellen's husband and Barbara's father. What kind of a man do you think I am? I'd have done the same thing." He dropped into the swivel chair and leaned back from the steel desk. "We've got to think this out, Wes. We can't afford a mistake."

"God, no," Malone said.

"The first problem is Ellen and Barbara. And you, if you go back."

"No if, John. I can't leave them there alone."

Secco nodded slowly. His face reflected his father's pastures, full of steel ruts and the patience of livestock. "The question is, Wes, how to capture those three without endangering the lives of you and your family."

"That isn't the question at all," Malone said. "I started out thinking that way, too. It can't be done."

The chief seemed about to argue. But he did not. "What do you mean it can't be done?"

"There's no way," Malone said. "Believe me, John. As long as they've got the guns and Ellen and Bibby there's no way. Any move we make they'll shoot them. Or threaten to unless we let them make a getaway, using Ellen and Bibby as shields. Either way they're goners. Furia's got nothing to lose. He's in for one murder, he may as well be in for three or four. You don't know this man, John. Any way this thing winds up, Furia's going to go out shooting. I doubt he can be taken alive."

Secco said quietly, "What do you suggest, Wes?"

"The money. Give him the money."

Secco looked away.

"Get it out of the safe deposit box. If you talk to him, maybe Judge Trudeau will play ball. He owes you, John, if not for you he'd never have made judge. So get Trudeau's order and get the money out of the box and offer Furia the twenty-four thousand in exchange for Ellen and Bibby. Give him a safe conduct and time for a getaway. The money is what he wants. It's the only deal he'll make."

Malone stopped, exhausted.

The chief said nothing.

"You won't buy it," Malone said.

"No, I won't, Wes. Do you know why?"

"Why?"

"Because it's not in my power to do what you want. That payroll belongs to Aztec."

"The hell with Aztec!"

"It's not that simple," Secco said. "I guess I'd feel the way you do if I were in your spot, Wes. But I have the legal responsibility. Even if I were willing to do it, it isn't my money to dispose of."

"Then put it up to Curtis Pickney! What the hell is twenty-four thousand dollars compared to two lives? Even Pickney ought to be able to see that!"

"It doesn't belong to Pickney, either. It belongs to his company. It really wouldn't be Aztec's decision, either. They're insured against robbery and theft, so it's the insurance company that's holding the bag. Can you see an insurance company authorizing a deal with a payroll robber at their own expense? Wes, you're dreaming. If you weren't so desperate you'd realize it."

"You've got to do this for me, John," Malone said hoarsely. "I don't care whose money it is. If I could borrow twenty-four thousand dollars from the bank or a personal finance company I'd do it in a shot, even if it meant going into hock for the rest of my life. But you know Wally Bagshott or nobody would lend a man with my salary and no collateral that kind of money. Even selling my house wouldn't do any good, I have less than six thousand dollars' equity in it. That Aztec payroll is all I've got to bargain with! John, for God's sake."

John Secco shook his head. His eyes were screwed up as if the sun were in them.

"You won't do it for me." Malone cracked his knuckles, not knowing he was doing it. "The first time I've ever asked you or anybody for a goddam thing and you won't do it!"

"I can't do it," Secco said. "I'm the police officer in charge of law enforcement in New Bradford, Wes, I've got a sworn duty. I can't take somebody else's money and make a dicker with a gang wanted for murder and robbery—I'd be open to indictment for conspiracy and grand larceny myself. And even if I did it, do you think this gang would trust a police chief to hold up his end of such a deal? They'd still take Ellen and Barbara as hostages for their getaway. No, there's got to be some other way—"

The telephone rang.

"Yes?" Secco said. His face turned to stone. "Yes, he's here, Ellen."

Malone gaped.

"Wes." Secco held out the phone.

"Ellen," Malone said in a whisper. "What is it?"

"I've been trying to reach you all over town." He did not recognize her voice, it was inhuman, something out of a machine. "They've left."

"Left."

"Furia got nervous. He decided he couldn't trust you. That woman worked on him. So they left. They took Bibby with them."

"Let me get this." Malone ran the back of his hand over his forehead. "They took Bibby . . ."

Now she was crying.

"Honey. Please. Did they say where to make contact with them? Did they go back to the cabin at the Lake?"

"I don't know, Loney, I don't know . . ."

"Ellen, you've got to stop crying a minute, I've got to know exactly what they said. They must have said something."

"Furia said you're to have the money by noon tomorrow here in the house and wait with it till they get in touch with us he didn't say when and no police he said or we'll never see Bibby again, not even her body, it's our last chance he said . . ."

"I'll be home as soon as I can."

Malone hung up.

"I heard it," Chief Secco muttered. "I'll give you all the time you want, Wes, I won't make a move or say a word to anybody about this without your permission and if there's any way I can help, I mean except . . ."

"Go to hell," Malone said, and walked out.

He made his approach with the old stealth knowing it was unnecessary and hoping it was necessary but they were gone except for a garbage can full of empty food tins and liquor bottles and some filthy dishes in the sink.

Malone searched the cabin for a clue, anything that might tell him where they had gone. There was nothing and for a time he went out of his mind, he did everything in a trance of fury, blundering through underbrush and kicking cabin doors in and racing up and down dirt roads along the Lake looking for a sign of life, a smudge against the sky, a car in the bushes, anything.

Afterward, in the dusk, he drove the Saab slowly back to town.

First I had the money but lost Bibby.
Then I got Bibby back but lost the money.
Now I've lost both.

Saturday, Sunday, Monday, Tuesday

The Weakness

The house was cold. Malone turned up the thermostat but nothing happened. He went down into the cellar and pressed the emergency button on the stack and the furnace boomed. Afterward he could not remember anything about the heat, the cellar, or the furnace.

It had been a night to forget. Ellen had spent the day cleaning up the mess and getting things put back, and after Malone got home she cooked a dinner from something the visitors had left in the fridge and Malone could not remember what he had put in his mouth. He had not wanted to go to bed, saying "Suppose . . ." but Ellen rapped his lips with her finger and stripped his shirt and pants off and his underwear and socks and got him into his pajamas as if he were a child. As if he were Bibby. She tucked him in and crept in beside him and for the first time Malone cried. He kept jerking as if under a whip and Ellen tightened her arms and legs about him and murmured mothering sounds until, like a child, he fell asleep.

When he fell asleep Ellen got out of bed and shuffled to Barbara's room. She spent the rest of the night sitting in Barbara's little rocker with Miss Twitchit in her lap. Once she sang the soft song she had made up before Bibby could even crawl, not the tune really, it was let's face it the Brahms *Lullaby*. I couldn't make up a tune Ellen used to say with a laugh I'm practically tone-deaf. But the words were her own, hush and baby and love, words that came from her womb.

She woke up in a nasty dawn and found that she was crying. When she was over it she put Miss Twitchit back in her doll cradle that Loney had made from a broken-down rocker of his mother's and only then did she go back to the big bedroom and stretch out beside her husband. She lay on the edge of the bed so as not to disturb him. When she heard him grunt and sit up she made sure to have her eyes shut.

Thank God she's getting a decent sleep.

At first Goldie was all for lighting out, even before they came back for the kid.

"It's getting more and more risky, Fure. I don't like this hanging around New Bradford."

"The payroll," Furia said.

"I know, but what's the sense being mules about it when we're hot for a murder rap? There are plenty other payrolls around. So we take our lumps on this one. I say let's scramble and lose ourselves in the scenery. We ought to get out of the state. Maybe hit for Kansas or Indiana, those farmers out there are sitting ducks."

"I ain't leaving here without the bread," Furia said, and from the way he said it Goldie knew that she had better clam up, her skin was starting to itch again.

She picked the emergency holeup after they got the kid back. The shack they had rented at Balsam Lake was out of the question, they agreed on that, but Furia wanted to bust into one of the other cabins, maybe at the other end of the Lake, he was in a rotten mood and it took special methods to work him out of it. Goldie worked him out of it on the bed in the shack they were abandoning after she did what he liked best, which Hinch had watched through a good crack in the door, it was his favorite. Hinch was supposed to be guarding the kid, Furia had told him to, but he enjoyed their wrestling holds when he could do a Peeping Tom without getting caught. Anyways the kid was too scared to try anything, she was right there with him in the kitchen shivering on a chair, he could hear her teeth going clackety-clack without turning around.

"The Lake is the first place he'll look, Fure, believe me," Goldie said, "as soon as he gets the message we grabbed the kid again. He'll tear up these woods. So it figures like we get out of here fast and settle in where he can look all year long and he won't find us. We oughtn't to have come back to this shack at all. What's the sense having to cool him before you get the money back?"

"Okay, okay," Furia said dreamily, "I buy it."

Hinch was making faces at the kid for kicks when they came out of the bedroom.

They spotted the Saab with Malone at the wheel hell-bent for the Lake, he was hunched over blind, he passed the Chrysler without a look.

"What did I tell you?" Goldie said with a laugh. "Drive on, Stinkfoot."

The house she had picked was at the other side of town, near the town line of Tonekeneke Falls but well away from both centers, standing by itself on a back road a good hundred yards in and hidden by shade trees taller than the house. You could pass it a thousand times and never know it was here, Goldie said. Which is a fact, Furia said with satisfaction.

There was even a flagstoned patio out back and an outdoor pool with a heater attachment, but the pool was drained for the winter, too bad, Furia said, we could have had ourselves a dunk like the richbitches.

The place was owned by a New York family who used it for summers and long holiday weekends the rest of the year. Goldie knew about it because her sister Nanette had mentioned the Thatchers in her letters, she was their regular summer baby-sitter, they went out a lot. They had three impossible children but Nanette said they paid her twice the going rate so who's kicking. There was no chance of the Thatchers showing up all of a sudden because they had traipsed off to Europe till after the Christmas holidays, that's how the other half lives.

Furia approved. Aside from the money he was feeling great after Goldie's special treatment and when Hinch broke through the back door and Goldie locked Barbara in the downstairs maid's room he didn't even get mad at the furnace, it wouldn't go on, the tanks must need oil. Maybe they don't pay their bills, he cracked.

He went around admiring. The country furniture was

108

kingsize and handfinished, white pine treated with just linseed oil, all dowels, not a nail in them. The fieldstone fireplace in the living room was almost tall enough for Hinch to walk into and there were genuine oil paintings on the walls. Though Furia took a dim view of the paintings. They look like cripples did them a skillion years ago, he said, and look how they're all browned up and full of cracks. There was even a big-screen color TV set in a special white pine cabinet which right away Goldie turned on, but Furia said, "The hell with that, we got to listen to what's going on around here," and he turned off the TV and turned on the radio, a kingsize transistor, standing on the mantelpiece. He tuned in the station at Tonekeneke Falls, there was a rock combo on, and he left it on while he went exploring.

The country kitchen made him do a little dance like Hitler. It was all of pine and brick with a regular Rockette lineup of gleamy copper pots and skillets on wrought iron racks hanging from the beams, like a color spread in *House Beautiful* or something. "Would this 'a' bugged my old lady's eyes out! What she had to cook in shouldn't happen to a dog. When she had something to cook." The refrigerator was empty, but there was a twenty-cubic-foot freezer loaded with steaks and roasts and other great stuff and a for-real cooking fireplace with a black iron door at the back that opened into something Goldie said they called a Dutch oven big enough to do a whole lamb in and a black iron pot hanging on a black iron dohinky that swung out in the damnedest way. "Man, that pot's bigger than my old lady's washtub," Furia said, practically smiling, "you sure can pick 'em, Goldie."

He felt so good that when Hinch found a room lousy with books from floor to ceiling and a white pine bar full of bottles of the best stuff and poured himself a waterglass of Black Label, Furia let him. "Live it up, Hinch, have yourself a grin." But then he had to show what a big man he was, he said, "What the hell is the kid bawling for? I'll give her something to bawl," and he unlocked the door to the maid's room and slapped the little girl around some, not much, he pulled his punches, he had nothing against kids, but it only made her bawl louder. "What's with this little punk?" Furia said disgustedly. "You'd think being her old man is fuzz she'd be used to getting banged around, give her some booze, Goldie, and shut her up." So Goldie got a couple slugs of Jack Daniels into Barbara and after

109

a while she stopped crying and fell asleep on the bed with her mouth open, snoring like a little lush. Furia got a charge out of that and when he locked her back in he was smiling again.

He kicked off his shoes and stretched out on the pine-and-cowhide sofa in the living room like the little king. "Think I'll have me a couple filly minyons for supper tonight, Goldie," Furia said. "Can you make 'em like the fat cats do, in that kitchen fireplace?"

"Don't see why not," Goldie said, "though I can't barbecue them, I don't see any charcoal."

"What the hell difference? Medium well, Goldie, can you do medium well in a fireplace?"

"Coming up," Goldie said, she was certainly anxious to please these days, "if Stinkfoot 'll get me a load of kindling and firewood. I saw a woodshed out back that's stacked."

But by this time Hinch had finished the fifth and thrown it through the mirror behind the bar.

"He shouldn't ought to done that," Furia said, "not a highclass dump like this. Hinch?"

"I heard her," Hinch said, coming in from the den. His face was white and his nose red, his eyes bugging. He looked steamy. "I ain't lugging no wood for her, I ain't her nigger."

"That shows how ignorant you are," Goldie said. "You have to say Negro or black."

"Nigger nigger nigger," Hinch said. "I ain't hauling no wood for nobody, special not for her."

"How about for me?" Furia asked.

"I don't feel so good," Hinch said, and sat down on the floor suddenly.

"You ain't used to fat cat booze is why," Furia said indulgently. "It's my fault for letting you. What the hell, Goldie, I'll get the wood," and to her surprise he sprang off the sofa and trotted out on his stockinged feet. She almost called after him it's a dirt floor out there but didn't, you never knew with Fure and things were going too good. She heard the back door open and stay open.

Goldie went into the downstairs bathroom which was all tiled in black and white real tiles and used the black porcelain john, it made her feel like a movie queen squatting there. Christ I'm going to live this way and no fooling, it's the only life. Soon as I shake Fure and that smelly Hinch.

She was primping her hair in the bathroom mirror which had the cutest little frosted bulbs set all around the frame à la Hollywood stars' dressing rooms when she jumped a foot. She had never heard such a scream except in the movies. It was like a police siren going off in her ear or a pig getting stuck, she remembered that from when she was a little girl and sneaked off to Hurley's chicken farm after her old man against orders just to watch what they did to the pigs. When the sound turned all bubbly she could practically see it choking on its blood.

She made it to the woodshed before Hinch, who had trouble getting off the floor.

Furia was backed off in a corner of the shed chucking firewood in every direction while his mouth opened and closed and nothing came out. The shed was full of furry things jumping and dodging. His eyes were dropping out of his head, the corners of his nose were blue. There was drool coming out of his mouth.

"Rats . . ."

Goldie couldn't believe her ears. She walked over to him and shook his arm hard.

"What are you talking about, Fure?" she said. "They're field mice."

"Rats," he panted. His tough little body felt like Jello under her hand.

"Fure, for Chrissake. I ought to know a field mouse when I see one. They used to run all over our kitchen in the Hollow. They won't hurt you."

"They went for me . . ."

"They couldn't do that. They're harmless."

"They bite . . ."

"Not people. They're grain eaters. Not like rats. See, they're all gone now." There was a hundred-pound sack stamped GOLDEN BULKY in the shed. The mice had gnawed holes in it, the dirt floor was honey brown where they had burrowed. "The Thatchers must keep a horse here summers. This is horse feed, Fure, that's what they were after, not you."

He didn't believe her. He kept shivering and hugging himself.

Hinch was spreadlegged in the entrance with a puzzle written on his face. He was looking from Furia to the dirt floor of the shed and back again. Furia's wild heaves had struck two mice. One was lying with its head flattened out

111

in an omelet of blood and brains. The other was still alive, scrabbling with its forelegs as if its back were broken.

"You scared of these bitty things?" Hinch asked in a wondering voice.

Furia swallowed convulsively.

Hinch walked over to the wounded mouse with a grin and kicked. It flew up and against the back wall of the shed and fell like a shot. He picked it up by the tail and went back and picked up the other one by the tail and went back again and dangled the two dead mice inches from Furia's nose. Furia screeched and tried to climb the wall. Then he was sick all over the dirt. Goldie had to jump back.

"Be goddam if he ain't scared shitless," Hinch said. He walked out and threw the mice all the way over into the empty pool. It was as if Hinch had just learned that babies didn't come out of their mothers' armpits.

Furia couldn't get down more than a couple of mouthfuls even though Goldie did the steaks exactly the way he liked them. She almost laughed in his face.

She found it a gas too the way he kept hanging on to the fireplace poker, a five-footer with three prongs at the business end. His eyes had grown as quick as the mice, darting about the floor, especially in corners. He drank three cups of black coffee without letting go of the poker.

Barbara woke up whimpering and Furia got ugly. "Shut that brat's yap or so help me Jeese I'll ram this thing down her goddam throat."

"All right, Fure, all right," Goldie said, and found some powdered milk in the cupboard and stirred up a glass. She brought the child the milk and a piece of cold steak. Barbara sipped some of the milk but turned away from the meat, her eyes were rolling up, I guess I gave her too much of a slug, well, better drunk than dead. She finally dropped back to sleep.

"She won't bother you now," Goldie said, coming out.

"Cool it, big man," Hinch said with a wink. "A couple of lousy mice."

That was when Furia swung the long fire tool and ripped Hinch's cheek. If Hinch hadn't been so quick the prongs would have gone through to his tonsils. He looked astounded. Goldie had to swab the wound with antiseptic she found in the medicine chest, she swabbed good and hard, and she slapped one of those three-inch Band-Aids over it.

Hinch kept looking at Furia with his eyebrows humped up like questions.

Saturday morning passed in jerks like a film jumping its sprockets. Malone wandered about the house picking things up and setting them down as if to satisfy himself that they were still there. The next thing he was taking in the milk. The milk brought Bibby into focus and he shut the refrigerator door as reverently as if it were the lid of a coffin. When Ellen set breakfast before him he simply sat and looked at it. He did not even drink the coffee. She finally took the dishes away.

Ellen had mourning under her eyes, bands of dark gray. Once she said, "Noon. What happens after noon, Loney?"

He turned away. He resents my reminding him. As if he needs reminding. What a thing to say, now of all times. Why am I so good to him at night and so bitchy daytimes?

But she's my child.

My lost, my frightened baby.

They sat in the parlor, he on the sofa, she on the rocker, watching the little cathedral clock on the mantel. When noon came they both sat up straight, as if at a call. When the clock stopped striking it was like a death.

Ellen began to cry again.

Malone jumped up and ran out into Old Bradford Road leaving the front door open. It was a mean day and the meanness slid into the house. He stood in the middle of the empty street staring in the direction of Lovers Hill. The Cunninghams' mongrel bitch came trotting up and licked his hand. Malone wiped his hand on his pants and went back into the house, shutting the door this time. Ellen was upstairs, he heard her moving about in one of the bedrooms.

Bibby's I'll bet.

He sank onto the sofa again and placed his hands uselessly on his knees, looking at the clock. When John Secco drove up it was twenty minutes of two and Malone was still sitting there.

Secco came in his own car, a three-year-old Ford wagon with no markings. He was in civvies.

"No sense getting your neighbors wondering," the chief said. He had more than midafternoon shadow and Malone

113

doubted he had shaved. For some reason it made him angry. "Ellen, I know how this has hit me, I can imagine what you're going through." Ellen said nothing. "Been a call? Letter, message?"

"Nothing," Malone said.

"Well, it's early. Could be they're putting some pressure on. Or giving you plenty of time to play ball."

"With what?" Ellen said. Secco was silent. "I knew that's what you'd do, Loney."

"Do what?" Malone said.

"Tell the whole thing to John. You promised you wouldn't. I told you I'd walk out on you if you did."

"Wes did the only thing," Secco said. "Do you suppose I'd put your little girl in danger, Ellen?"

"I don't know."

"I thought you considered me your friend."

"You're a policeman."

"I'm also a husband and a father. You ought to know me better than that."

"I don't know anything any more."

"Do you want me to leave?" the chief asked.

They waited a long time. Finally Ellen's mouth loosened and she said, "John, we don't know what to do, where to turn."

"That's why I'm here, Ellen. I want to help."

"Sure," Malone said. "Get me that money."

"Ask me something that's possible, Wes. Anyway, I think there's something we can do."

"Without the twenty-four thousand?" Malone laughed. "Furia thinks I've lifted it. You figured out a way to convince him I didn't?"

"I've been thinking over what you told me, I mean about what you did on your own." Secco seemed to be picking his way through the available words and choosing only the finest. "Maybe when they rented that cabin at the Lake last summer they at the same time rented a second cabin as a backup just in case. I thought it worth a try."

Malone raised his head. "I never thought of that."

"Only they didn't. I've spent the day so far doing another check of the real estate offices." He added quickly, "Don't worry. I didn't tip the hand."

Malone slumped back. Ellen just sat there.

"All the other possibilities were either vacated as of Labor Day or they're rented the year round by people who are known. So wherever they've dug in this time it's likely not at the Lake. It could be anywhere, out of the county even. It would take a hundred men—"

"You mustn't do that!" Ellen cried.

"Ellen, I told you. I wouldn't take chances with Barbara's safety."

"All I know is I want my baby back."

"Isn't that what we all want? Look. Wes, you listening?"

"I'm listening," Malone said.

"This woman who hijacked the payroll, Goldie. She could be working with Furia against the other man, Hinch, to squeeze Hinch out. They could be both putting on an act for Hinch's benefit."

"Damn," Malone said. "I never thought of that, either."

"But I doubt it. From what you told me about the way Furia acted when they were here in your house, it's likelier she's doublecrossing the two of them the way you doped it."

"Round and round we go," Malone said.

"No, listen." Chief Secco leaned forward in his effort to hold them, they slipped away so easily. "The way you described this Hinch, Wes, he seemed to be the weak sister of the three, a dumb character."

"He hasn't a brain in his head."

"The dumb ones of a gang are the ones to go after. In this case, from what you say, the groundwork with Hinch has already been laid."

"How do you mean?"

"You told me that the first time they came here—when they first took Barbara—Furia told Hinch to meet them at the cabin and Hinch was upset, you got the impression he was worried they might run out on him."

"So?"

"You also said that the second time they came, after you got Barbara back, when you told them the money'd been stolen from the house and Ellen accused Furia of having been the one, Hinch seemed half convinced it was true. That's what I mean by the groundwork being laid. He doesn't trust Furia. He's already got his doubts. Suppose we could convince him."

"That Furia took the money? But he didn't, John. Goldie Vorshek took it."

"We know that and the Vorshek woman knows it, but Hinch and Furia don't." There was nothing in the chief's voice or manner to suggest that he was about to sell something, he was being very careful about that. "If we can get Hinch to believing that Furia is playing him for a sucker, even a bear of little brain like that is going to start thinking of his own hide. It's a cinch he's in this thing for his cut of the loot. If there's no cut for him he's going to want out. The only way Hinch could get out now is by making a deal with us, in his own interest and to get back at the partner taking him for a ride. He'll make contact. He'll tell us where they're hiding. He might even help us when we close in. That's the way I figure it."

"And that's the way my Bibby would get killed," Ellen said. "Absolutely no."

"Ellen," Secco said. "Would Barbara be in more danger than she is right now if they got to distrusting one another? She might even be in less, because if the plan worked out Hinch would have a personal interest in seeing she stays safe. He'd know what would happen to him if he let Furia hurt her." Secco took out his pipe and fiddled with it. He put it back in his pocket. "Look, I'm not saying this is guaranteed. There are a lot of ifs when you're dealing with dangerous morons like these. But as things stand, Furia won't give up Barbara without the money, if then—I have to be frank with you, Ellen—and we don't have the money to give them. You've got to accept how things are, not how you'd like them to be."

Ellen was giving her head little stubborn shakes.

"But, of course, you've got to make the decision. I don't have the right to make it for you. Even if I had, I wouldn't."

"The answer is no," Ellen said.

"Ellen." There was a hint of life in Malone's eyes. "Maybe John has something. God knows we don't. Maybe such a trick . . ."

"No."

"Wait. John, how would you get to Hinch? What do you have in mind?"

"Wherever they're hiding out it's a sure thing they've got a radio. So that's our channel of communication. Manufactured story, some cooked-up announcements on the air, I don't know, I haven't laid it out yet. But the point is, if we can get the right message through to him—"

"But Furia and this Goldie would hear it, too."

"Let them. It would make her more jittery than she already is, a doublecross inside the gang is the last thing she wants the other two to start kicking around. And as far as Furia's concerned, it puts him on the defensive with Hinch and that could make them go for each other's throats. It's a tactic that's broken up a lot of gangs. But as I say, I can't make the decision for you people. She's your flesh and blood."

"It's up to you, Ellen," Malone said. "What do you say?"

"Oh, God."

Secco got up and went to the window. He took out his pipe again and sucked on it emptily. His back said he wasn't there.

"Loney, help me, help me," Ellen moaned.

"Do you want me to make the decision?"

"I don't know, I don't know."

"You've got to know. There's no time for this, Ellen. Do I decide for both of us, or do you, or what?"

"They'll murder her, Loney."

"They may murder her anyway."

She stiffened as if he had struck her.

Ellen, Ellen, how else do you prepare yourself?

"Well?"

He could just hear her. "Whatever you say."

"John," Malone said.

Secco turned around.

"We go for broke."

It turned out that the chief had Harvey Rudd waiting in the wagon. "I brought Harvey along in case you said yes," Secco said. "He'll have to be briefed, Wes. I told him nothing."

Harvey Rudd was The Voice of Taugus Valley. He was an ex-Marine news broadcaster who had passed up a top job with a New York network to start an independent radio station, WRUD, in Tonekeneke Falls. He owned it, programed it, edited its news, sometimes took its mike, and he had been known to sweep it out. He was a fortyish Down Easter with a long Yank nose and a short Yank tongue.

Ellen said one thing in Rudd's presence. She said it to Chief Secco. "Can this man be trusted?"

When the chief said, "Yes," Ellen nodded and went upstairs, not to be seen again during the afternoon.

Rudd didn't say anything, not even with his eyes, which

were northern ocean blue and looked as if they belonged in a four-master's crow's-nest. They did not even express anything at the sight of the plaster on Malone's hair and the welt on his jaw. He set his surprising Texas-style white Stetson on the sofa beside him and waited.

Malone told the story leaving out nothing. The radio man listened without a word. When Malone was finished Chief Stecco told about using WRUD to get to Hinch. "Will you do it, Harvey?"

For the first time Malone heard Rudd's voice.

"I have two children of my own." Malone had expected a voice like a cheap guitar, like fellow-officer Sherm Hamlin's, Sherm had been born in Boothbay Harbor and had served as a guard at the prison in Thomaston before following his married daughter down to New Bradford, he had never lost his whangy accent. But this voice was more like one of Lawrence Welk's baritone saxes. "What exactly did you have in mind, John?"

"Well, I got an idea while Wes was filling you in. You could put on the air a series of those now—what d'ye call 'em?—like trailers, teasers, of a, say, radio drama. You know, like you were working up advance interest in a show you were going to run next week or month, give pieces of the plot. Like that. What we'd do is use the actual facts of this case, except we'd make out like the head man of the gang was doublecrossing the other two. The idea is to get Hinch to worrying ... No, Harvey?"

Rudd was shaking his head. "In the first place, John, WRUD doesn't run dramatic shows, they went out a long time ago on radio, so it would sound phony straight off to anybody who does any listening at all. Second, if this Hinch is as stupid as you say he is you're not going to get anything through his skull with subtlety. Third, from what Mr. Malone says, there's no time to prepare anything elaborate. Whatever's done has to be started right away— today, if possible."

"Then how would you handle it?"

"I'd do it on a straight news basis. It's something even a halfwit would understand and it would have the added advantage of sounding legitimate."

"You can't do that, Mr. Rudd," Malone said.

"Why not?"

"Because Furia would hear it, too. And he'd know that the only way such information could have gotten out was through me or my wife shooting our mouths off. That

118

would spell curtains for my little girl. He warned us to keep quiet or else. He's dangerous, Mr. Rudd, maybe even psycho. He means it. At least I can't take the chance that he doesn't."

"We can handle it so you and Mrs. Malone are put absolutely in the clear."

"How?"

"You leave that to me."

Malone's chin flattened. There was a pulse beating in the bruise. "I don't know. I'd have to think about it."

"Will you let me work on it, Mr. Malone? I promise not a word will go out over the air without your okay. Have you got a typewriter here?"

"No."

"Then just some paper," Rudd said easily, "I can't type worth a damn, anyway."

Malone went hunting for paper while he listened for a sign of life from upstairs and heard it, the creak-creak of the rocker in Barbara's room.

The kid was acting up again and Furia said give the little puke some more juice but Goldie said any more and she might get poisoned you want her alive don't you. She came up with a bottle of Sleep-Tite tablets she found in one of the upstairs bathrooms, so that problem was solved.

Furia ordered a top sirloin roast for his Saturday night dinner and Goldie had it thawing all day. The Thatchers had obliged by installing an electric spit in the old kitchen fireplace and Goldie built just the right fire, a slow one, to do the roast over. Furia spent a good twenty minutes watching it go round and round. I picked me a real cool broad, he said, fondly pinching her behind, I ought to set you up in the chow business, Goldie, I'll have that banana ripple ice cream for dessert they got in the freezer. Then he went back to the living room where Hinch was nursing an Old Crow on the rocks like a grudge, Furia had put him on short rations after the broken mirror, Hinch wasn't taking it as well as usual. Furia turned on the radio, which was set at WRUD, and stretched out on the sofa while Hinch brooded over at him.

There was the national news, then the news from the state capital, and Furia said to the radio come on, come on. Finally the announcer, who had a voice like a saxophone, said: "And now for the Taugus Valley news.

"First Selectman Russ Fairhouse urged residents of New Bradford today to support the Jaycee cleanup campaign, Operation Civic Pride. 'Please join your neighbors,' Mr. Fairhouse pleaded, 'in picking up gum wrappers and such and ridding our town of unsightly junk like abandoned old cars and washing machines and any other thrown-out items that may be laying around your property causing eyesores. Your administration is doing its part repairing the highway signs defaced mostly by teenagers the past summer, please do yours and impress on your children that in the end the cost of such vandalism is borne by you, the taxpayer.'

"A two-car accident on The Pike one mile north of Tonekeneke Falls today took the life of nineteen-year-old Alison Springer of Southville and sent three other teenagers to the New Bradford Hospital with critical injuries. State police say that the cars were engaged in a drag race.

"There has been no progress in the statewide hunt for the two holdup men who shot Thomas F. Howland to death and stole the Aztec Paper Products Company's payroll Wednesday night, according to Colonel Doug Pearce of the state police. 'It's my belief,' Colonel Pearce told WRUD today, 'that they made it out of the state. An All Points went out to authorities in adjoining states yesterday.' "

"Aha," Furia said with a grin. "They sure freaked out. Hear that, Hinch?"

"So what," Hinch grumbled. "We ain't got the bread."

"And now for today's Lighter-Side-of-the-News item," the saxophone continued with a chuckle in it. "There's another mystery of sorts in New Bradford that for a while today had Police Chief John Secco and his department thinking they were in the middle of a crime wave.

"A twelve-year-old boy named Willie, who runs a paper route in the Lovers Hill section of New Bradford delivering the New Bradford *Times-Press,* came into police headquarters this morning to report a crime. Willie claimed that on Thursday afternoon, while he was delivering his papers on his bicycle at the upper end of Old Bradford Road, he witnessed—in Willie's own words—'a short skinny guy with like a stocking over his head' sneaking into one of the houses. According to Willie, he promptly hid behind a rhododendron bush across the road and watched.

120

'The man came scooting out after a while,' Willie said, 'and he was carrying a little black bag that he didn't have when he went in—' "

"What the hell." Hinch sat up.

"Shut up, let's hear this!" Furia hissed.

" '—and he took off the stocking and beat it down the road.' Willie alleges that he followed the mysterious man and saw him turn into Lovers Hill with the black bag and head for the center of town still on foot."

Hinch was looking at Furia with his mouth open. Furia was on his feet glaring at the radio.

"Willie, who wears thick glasses, could give no description of the man beyond his short height and skinniness. Chief Secco was doubtful about the story on the face of it, since no housebreaking was reported Thursday and Willie, it seems, has a reputation for an overactive imagination. Nevertheless, the chief sent Officer Harry Rawlson to Old Bradford Road with the boy, who pointed out the house he claimed the man had burgled. It turned out that Chief Secco's doubts were all too justified. It was the home of a member of the New Bradford force, Officer Wesley Malone. Officer Malone, who has been off duty for a few days, said that he and Mrs. Malone had had no visitors at all on Thursday, illegal or otherwise, and that in any event nothing was missing. Mrs. Malone confirmed this, stating that they had never owned a little black bag. 'Willie either made a mistake about the house,' Officer Malone told his fellow-officer, 'or he's been reading too many mystery stories.' A check of the other houses on Old Bradford Road produced no confirmation of Willie's story, and he was sent home after a fatherly lecture by Chief Secco.

"Thus endeth New Bradford's latest excitement.

"Funeral services will be held tomorrow at two P.M. at Christ Church, Stonytown, for—"

Furia jabbed the radio off. When he turned around he saw Goldie standing in the doorway from the kitchen.

"What was that all about?" Goldie said.

"Nothing!" Furia said.

"Thursday afternoon," Hinch said slowly. "Small skinny guy. That fuzz and his old lady were telling the truth. I'll be goddam."

"Don't look at me!" Furia yelled. "It wasn't me! I was in the shack, damn it. I didn't even have the car, so how would I get into town?"

121

"Neither did the skinny guy," Hinch said. "He walked, this Willie said."

"So it was some local," Goldie said, "the way Malone said. There are lots of small skinny guys in this world. Looks to me, Fure, like this really ties it. Why don't we give it up as a bad job?"

"No," Furia said. "*No*."

"How do you expect Malone to get the money back when he doesn't even know who took it?"

"That's his problem!"

"You could 'a' walked," Hinch said, "it ain't that far. I hoofed it easy the night we pulled the heist."

"Maybe it was you!"

"Small, skinny," Hinch said. "Do I look small and skinny? Anyways, Fure, I wouldn't do that."

"And I would?"

Hinch did not reply. He was looking into his empty glass and frowning.

"Well, at least Malone and his wife didn't blow the whistle, you scared 'em good," Goldie said brightly. She was scratching one hand with the other. After a while she said, "The roast won't be long now. No potatoes or I'd make you some French fries, Fure. What vedge do you want?"

Furia told her what she could do with her vedge.

"I still think it's taking useless chances to hang around here," Goldie said. "Specially now that we know somebody did hijack the payroll. What do you say we write it off, Fure? We could be somewhere opening a bank and like grabbing us a real pile, not some snotty twenty-four grand."

"What do you think, Hinch?" Furia asked suddenly.

Hinch looked up.

"You think we ought to cut out, like Goldie says?"

Hinch got to his feet. He seemed to go up and up indefinitely. Goldie took one look at the expression on his face and stepped back into the kitchen.

"I think," Hinch said deliberately, "I'm going to make myself another drinkee."

Fure was uptight all Saturday evening, brooding over at Hinch getting smashed in his corner.

Furia had his right hand stuck under his coat like Napoleon. But he wasn't dreaming of new worlds to conquer, he wanted the Colt in his shoulder holster handy just in case, at least that was Goldie's analysis. This whole thing is a bust why did I ever tie in with these cockamamies? Better watch your step, girl, this could wind up with fireworks.

There was almost a fight over the TV. Furia wanted the TV on, Hinch wanted the radio on. The nine o'clock movie was a remake of *The Maltese Falcon,* I like that old fat guy, Furia said, he's real cool. Goldie said he's also been real dead for years it's somebody else in this version, why doesn't Hinch take the radio into the den then everybody's happy. Hinch said to hell with you bitch I like it right here. Furia said I want to see Humphrey Bogart and that's it and Goldie said he's dead too, Fure. Fure said according to you everybody's dead and Hinch said in a peculiar way so let that be a lesson to you. And he wasn't looking at Goldie when he said it. Goldie decided to go to the bathroom in case the argument heated up.

In the end Hinch took the radio into the den and Furia watched his movie. He kept complaining all through that it stank I liked the fat guy and Bogey better.

But Goldie noticed that he turned his chair so he could keep one eye on the den.

Come eleven o'clock there was Furia standing in the doorway of the den.

"What you listening to?" he asked Hinch.

"What do you think?" Hinch said. There were about three fingers left in the bottle of Smirnoff's.

"At the signal it will be exactly eleven o'clock," the announcer said. "This is Station WRUD, the Voice of Taugus Valley. Now for the news."

"What do you got to listen to the news for?" Furia said. "We heard it on the six o'clock."

"You don't want to hear it don't," Hinch said. "Me, I want to hear it."

"They didn't find us, if that's what you're worried about," Furia said. Hinch said nothing. "That's a joke, son."

Hinch said nothing.

Furia stayed where he was, looking at Hinch. He kept his hand under his coat.

Goldie turned the TV off in the living room so she could listen, too. From the living room.

National news. Statewide news. Then the saxophone voice said, "One of the three teenagers injured in today's two-car accident at Tonekeneke Falls which took the life of nineteen-year-old Alison Springer of Southville died this evening at the New Bradford Hospital. He was Kelly Wilson, Junior, eighteen, of Haddison. The two surviving teenagers are still listed in critical condition.

"Review of the additional salary upgradings proposed for New Bradford town employees last week has been completed, First Selectman Russ Fairhouse announced today, and the revised salary schedule will be brought before a town meeting next Friday night at eight P.M. in the New Bradford High School cafeteria.

"A combined meeting of the Women's Auxiliaries of the fire department of Taugus Valley will be held Monday evening at eight o'clock at the home of Mrs. Jeanine Lukenberry of Stonytown to complete plans for the joint pre-Christmas rummage sale for the benefit of Better Fire Prevention."

"Aaaa, turn it off," Furia said. "Who's interested in that crap?"

"I am," Hinch said, not moving.

"—a footnote to the Lighter-Side-of-the-News item we broadcast on our six o'clock news," the baritone sax was playing.

"See what I mean?" Hinch said. "You got to wait for the good stuff. What's the matter, Fure, you nervous?"

"Listen here, you—"

"Shut up," Hinch said quietly, "I want to hear this."

Furia's ear-points began to turn red. But he shut up.

"—seems that Willie is a persistent little cuss," the voice chuckled. "When Chief John Secco sent him home this afternoon, Willie didn't go home. He went back to Old Bradford Road and, as he told WRUD's Lighter-Side-of-the-News reporter this evening, 'I scouted around, they don't believe me about the man with the stocking over his face I'll prove it to 'em, I seen him throw that stocking away.' To everyone's surprise but Willie's he did just that. He went back to New Bradford police headquarters with a woman's nylon stocking which he claimed he found under the privet hedge in front of Officer Wesley Malone's house, where the alleged housebreaking took place. Chief Secco sent an officer over to the Malone place with the stocking, and Mrs. Malone identified it as one of hers which she had had drying on her clothesline and which had disappeared days ago. 'It must have been Rags that did it, she's the Cunninghams' dog next door, she's always

124

stealing things off my line," Mrs. Malone told the officer. Willie was sent home with a personal escort, Officer Mert Peck. Officer Peck advised Willie's father to take Willie on a tour of the woodshed, which Willie's father said he sure as heck was going to do. Please don't report any howling you may hear from that section of New Bradford. It's just Willie learning that free enterprise doesn't always pay.

"In one minute the music of the Taugus Rock Quarriers. But first, a message from—"

Hinch snapped the radio off. He turned about and began a leisurely survey of Furia. Furia's hand dug deeper under his coat.

"Hinch," Furia said. "I don't know from no stocking. That's the word."

"If you say so, Fure." Hinch held out the Smirnoff. "Need a little snort?"

Furia snarled, "That'll be the day," and backed out.

Furia looked up the Malones' number in the book and dialed.

Right away Malone's voice said hoarsely, "Yes?"

"It's me," Furia said. "Don't bother trying to trace this call, fuzz, it's a public booth a long ways from you. Well?"

"I haven't got it," Malone said. "For God's sake, I told you and told you. Look, there was a boy in town here who saw the thief sneak into my house Thursday and come out with the black bag—"

"I know, we heard it on the radio," Furia said. "You and your missus played it cool, that was smart, fuzz. But I don't care who took it. I want it back."

"I told you—! How is my little girl?"

"She's okay. So far. Did you think I was kidding, Malone? I want that bread or you never see your kid again."

"How am I supposed to do it? Why don't you get it through your head that you lost out on this deal through no fault of anybody and let Barbara go?"

"No dice," Furia said. "Look, it don't have to be the payroll. I ain't particular. Any twenty-four grand'll do. Work on it, Malone. I'll call you."

"Damn you, where would I get—?"

Furia hung up and stepped from the booth outside the railroad station. It was Sunday morning and Freight Street

125

looked like Gary Cooper's town at high noon. When he turned around there was Hinch.

"What are you doing here?" Furia snarled. "I thought I told you to stay in the house."

"Cabin fever," Hinch said.

Furia hesitated.

"I took the car, too," Hinch said. "You want to make something of it?"

Furia began to walk.

Hinch swung into step. The crease between his pink eyes had smoothed out.

"I'll give you a ride back," Hinch said. "If you say please?"

"I should never have listened to you," Malone stormed. "I should have told him Goldie had it and about the safe deposit box while I had him on the phone."

"That would have queered the whole setup, Wes," John Secco said. "You heard Furia. It's working. They've swallowed Rudd's bait hook and linc. That means it's stewing around in Hinch's head. He can't possibly have missed it, dumb or not. Give him a chance. When he's finally made up his mind that Furia crossed him he'll call in for a deal."

"But Goldie—"

"You said yourself she'd talk Furia out of it if you accused her. Then the whole thing might be shot. Don't go complicating things now, Wes. Have a little patience."

"But I can prove it to him!"

"How?"

"I forgot about the keys. When you rent a safe deposit box you get your own key, even a duplicate. So she's got two keys to a Taugus National safe deposit box. All Furia has to do is search her and that's it for Goldie."

"Do you think a woman like that would be fool enough to keep them on her, Wes? She's hidden them somewhere. That was the first thing I thought of." Secco shook his head. "Go up to Ellen."

Malone went upstairs. Ellen was in bed with a slight fever. She had an icebag on her forehead and her eyes were closed.

He sat down and thought of Barbara. Everything else was boiling around.

Chief Secco sucked on his pipe downstairs beside the telephone.

Thank God I was raised the son of a farmer.

A farmer grew patience the way he grew grass.

The call came two hours before daylight on Tuesday morning. Secco was sleeping on the cot in the kitchen near the wall extension, Malone on the sofa in the parlor beside the phone. He had it off the cradle before it rang twice. Secco was a breath behind picking up the extension.

"Hello?" Malone said.

"This Malone?" It was the cougar voice, the cougar voice, pitched in a mutter.

"Yes? Yes?"

"This is Hinch. You know. Look, I can't talk long, I had to wait till they were corked off good before I could use the phone. I'll make a deal."

"Yes?"

"I want out. I'll turn state's evidence. Do I get a deal?"

"Yes," Malone said, "yes."

Secco came running in noiselessly. He put his lips to Malone's ear and whispered, "Ask him where they are."

"Yes," Malone said again. "Where is the house?"

"I don't know where, I mean the street. Some crummy back road. It ain't far."

"Telephone number," Secco whispered.

"What's the phone number there?"

"7420."

"7420."

Secco wrote it down.

"Can you get my girl out of there, Hinch?"

"Fure took all the artillery. Anyways, Goldie's got her sleeping in with her and she locked the door."

"Then don't try anything. Stay put. We'll be out there. If you see a chance after we show, make a break for it with Barbara. Anything happens to my daughter it's no deal, Hinch, you get the book thrown at you. You hear me?"

"Yeah," Hinch muttered. He hung up.

Malone hung up.

He sat back and looked at the chief. Secco said briskly, "Don't sit there, Wes. Hand me the phone."

Malone handed it to him.

Secco dialed 411. It took a long time for the local

information operator to answer. He waited patiently. When she answered he said, "This is John Secco. Who's this, Margaret?"

"Sally, Chief."

"Sally. This is an emergency. Who in town has the number 7420?"

He waited again.

"Thanks, Sally. Keep quiet about this." He hung up. "It's on Maccabee Road, the Thatcher place. They closed it up for the winter. Wes?"

"I'm listening, John," Malone said.

"Why don't you go up and tell Ellen about this? I've got a police department to round up."

"John."

Secco stopped in the act of picking up the phone again. "What, Wes?"

"Maybe one man could get in and cover Furia before he can wake up—"

"You mean you."

"Give me a gun."

Secco shook his head. "You said yourself Furia sleeps like a cat, so no one man's going to take him in bed. Anyway, Wes, you're too involved, you'd be sure to mess it up. This is going to be a delicate business even with a squad. Let me handle it regulation procedure. It's the right way. The only way."

"She's my child—"

"And you're one of my officers, Wes. One of them."

"All right," Malone said. "But, John, I swear to you, if anything goes wrong—"

"How well have you done by yourself?" John Secco asked.

They stared at each other.

"Loney? What's going on down there?"

Malone went upstairs running away.

Tuesday

The Deal

Malone went into action chewing on doom. I have no part
or place in this, I'm the only one without a uniform or a
gun, John doesn't trust me, I should never have gone to
him, Ellen was right, it's not John's fault what else can he
do it's his job, the fault is all mine I had no business
becoming a cop. Being a cop is like being a Marine and
what kind of Marine did I make. I should have handled
this by myself all the way through. How could it have
come out worse than this?

They were a force of twenty-two men, eight New
Bradford officers besides Chief Secco and Malone, and a
dozen troopers. They were packing shotguns and carbines
and tear gas launcher attachments and gasmasks from the
state police barracks and enough ammunition to face
down a riot mob, no missing ingredient but the barri-
cades.

And all for what. They don't begin to realize the kind
of kill-crazy kook they're up against, a show of force like
this is going to put his back up like a skunk and make him
piss his stink, hc'll see all the dreams he dreamed of hate
and glory in whatever shit pile he was dragged up in come

130

true and he'll go out blazing away and taking Bibby with him and me too I'll be there I'll be there to go with her. And what Ellen gets out of the deal is two graves side by side in New Bradford Cemetery. Poor kid. You rate better.

Unless . . . unless Hinch wants to live more than he's scared of Furia. And wanting will find the brains he wasn't born with to figure out a way to get on top. Get the better of Furia before it's too late. You're my ace, Hinch. In this hole I'm in.

One man one vote. That's what it comes down to. Furia against Malone. Furia against Hinch. Not Furia against twenty-two law officers creeping up with funk in their mouths and guns in their hands.

"Don't worry, Wes," Chief Secco said. "It's going to be all right."

"Give me a written guarantee?"

"What you are and how you operate," Secco said. "That's the only guarantee there is, Wes."

There was no communication after that.

The cars were left a quarter mile from Maccabee Road and they made their professional approach in the predawn lugging their weapons and ammo and masks to the Thatcher place like a platoon of grunts on search-and-destroy, every man's face tight as a secret, every tongue tasting the death of somebody else. Can't John see that? They're disciplined and they're set to follow orders but let Furia draw blood and see what happens.

John John.

Bibby . . .

Come on Hinch.

Chief Secco's operational plan was an attack in force while the enemy's guard was down. Furia was not aware that his hideout was blown, he had no reason to post a lookout, they would have all the advantages of near darkness and a sleeping or sleepy foe, and overwhelming surprise would carry the day. A noiseless entry front and back, coordinated, the main group with rubbers over their shoes sneaking upstairs, Secco knew the old house well it was built in 1799 the chestnut floors were all creaked out and the stairs heavily carpeted . . . one burst into Furia's room, heave a couple of gas cans, and that would be it. The child was sleeping with the woman in another bedroom according to Hinch, an auxiliary force would handle that at the same time. The woman was too smart to try

131

anything foolish and Hinch was spoken for. If Furia elected or was able to shoot it out he would be blasted into a better world by a dozen guns before he could get his weapons up.

The sky was turning gray and there was just enough light to see by. Chief Secco had had the men synchronize their watches and every eye was on the second hand. There were eight men behind trees to the front of the house, eight men behind trees at the rear, and three men to each side hiding in shrubbery.

The men behind the house could see the back door broken half off its hinges where the gang had got in. The problem was the front door. It was shut and probably locked. They had debated whether to make entry in a body through the back door but decided to carry out the original plan. Sergeant Louis Lombard of the troopers had a picklock for tumbler locks and a can of 3-in-1 to oil the hinges as a precaution against squeaks. The men at the rear were to give him forty seconds to get the front door open before they made their move.

Six men were to remain on guard outside against the impossibility that the gunman might break away from the force inside.

How could it go wrong?

It did. At zero minus fifty seconds, Sergeant Lombard, allowing an extra ten seconds for his approach, ducked out from behind his tree. He was forty-three years old and he had a son fighting in Vietnam. He was a large man with large hands. In one he carried the oil can and the picklock, in the other his weapon. He ducked out from behind his tree and doubled over began to run on the balls of his feet across the lawn toward the front door. He was no more than a third of the way to the door when Furia shot him from a downstairs window, one-and-two-three. His favorite number. Because of the poor light the first shot missed Lombard's heart and smacked into the shoulder of the arm carrying the oil can and the picklock. The oil can and the picklock flew up and over his head. The second shot struck him in the business hand and the revolver went off from the convulsion of his trigger finger. The weapon dropped in a plumbline to the grass. The third shot zinged over his head and struck the tree behind which Malone was hiding. The sergeant became a crab, by instinct skittering on all fours away from his death, shat-

132

tered right hand between body and grass holding his shattered left shoulder.

For two seconds there was nothing but the morning. Then, as one man, as by an order heard in the blood, Chief Secco's army opened fire front and rear. Every window on the ground floor was a black hole in a moment.

They kept firing.

Sergeant Lombard reached the trees, gave Sherm Hamlin a white grin as Hamlin hauled him to safety, and passed out.

"Stop firing, stay under cover!" Secco was yelling. "Harry, work your way around to the back and tell them to stop firing there, too!"

Soon they stopped. A truce settled over the unconscious trooper's moans. One trooper ran back in the direction of the cars, another began to drag the wounded man away.

"They could have killed Bibby," Malone was saying brokenly, "maybe they did, John."

"No, she's all right, I tell you, I know she is." The seams in Secco's cheeks seemed rubbed with dirt. He grabbed a bullhorn. "Furia! Can you hear me?"

"I hear you." The call, a saucy spin, came from behind a wide crack in the front door. "Anybody else shoots and I blow the kid's head off. I got her right in front of me. Want to see?"

The door opened wider. The light was better now and Malone saw a small white valentine face with blank eyes like her doll's. Behind her crouched Furia. The Colt was jammed against her head, just behind the ear.

She's alive she's still alive. Hinch why don't you jump him from behind? Now.

"Nobody's going to shoot any more if you don't." The enlargement of Chief Secco's voice by the bullhorn gave it an almighty quality, stern, patient, paternal. "Furia, the house is surrounded by twenty-two police officers. You can't get away. You wouldn't have a prayer. Send Barbara out unharmed and toss out your guns. If you do that without any further resistance or bloodshed the district attorney says he'll take it into account. You'll get the best break possible, I have the D.A.'s word on that. What do you say?"

Now Hinch while John does his thing.

The door banged open and Furia rose from his heels where he was squatting. He had Barbara about the waist with his left arm, holding her up before him. As the gunman straightened Secco grunted in surprise. Furia's face was covered by the Papa Bear mask.

So now you know what you're dealing with, John.

"You think you can con me with that D.A. crap?" Furia shouted through the mask. His right hand flourished the Colt, the Walther automatic was stuck in his waistband. "No more than Hinch. Your stooge is a Mr. No-Brains, don't you know that? He couldn't keep nothing from me, I'm way ahead of him, always was. I worked him over and it wasn't ten minutes ago I got out of him about that call to the kid's old man. I know all about your deals. Here's the only deal Hinch rates. And it's not from you, fuzz, it's from me."

Hinch appeared. His arms were jammed behind his back, apparently lashed together. A handkerchief had been shoved into his mouth, his own belt was the gag that secured it, nothing-sounds were coming out. His pants were halfway to his knees, he was wriggling like a go-go dancer from the waist down in a comical effort to keep them up without hands. His hair had turned a brighter shade of red that had run down his face and dripped onto his shirt. The same shade of red was dribbling from his mouth. One eye was closed and swollen a funereal purple-black.

"Go, man, go," Furia gurgled. He set his foot in the small of Hinch's back and kicked. Hinch staggered forward and fell on his face. He was up in an incredible acrobatics and hobbling furiously toward the trees. Furia leveled the Colt and shot him one-and-two-three. He stuck the Colt in his belt and whipped out the Walther. The child shielding him showed no expression.

"You wanted my answer, fuzz, there it is," the little man in the Papa Bear mask said. "Malone?"

"Here I am," Malone said.

"Wes, for God's sake!"

Malone stepped out from behind his tree.

"Here I am," Malone said again.

"Your fuzz buddies think I'm putting on an act," Furia said. "They think that's ketchup on Hinch and we're playing like in the movies. Go over to Hinch and tell your fuzz buddies that's real blood and he's real dead."

"Wes, he'll shoot you, too . . ."

Malone walked over to the grass to Hinch. Hinch lay on his face with his knees drawn under him as if he were

134

praying to Mecca. All three of Furia's bullets had gone into the back of his head, most of which was not there.

Malone looked around and nodded.

"Come back, Wes!"

"Stay there, Malone, I'm talking." Malone remained over Hinch's body. "Okay? Got the message? Now here's the rest of my answer. You fuzz sonsabitches out there blow. You're going to let me and my woman and Malone's kid ride out of here and you ain't going to raise a hand to stop us. I give you five minutes to make up your mind. If you ain't gone in five minutes, every mother's fuzz out there, I'll throw the kid out on top of Hinch without a head."

He stepped back with Barbara. The door all but closed.

Malone walked back to the trees.

"He means it," Secco said thoughtfully.

"Aren't you going to do it, John?" Malone asked.

Secco was silent.

"You've got to. He told you what he'd do to Bibby if you don't."

"He killed Tom Howland. He's shot Sergeant Lombard. He murdered this Hinch in front of my eyes."

"So you want him to add my daughter to his list?"

"Let's not go for each other, Wes. Even if I were willing I have no authority to order the troopers away. With Sergeant Lombard out of commission I'd have to get in touch with the barracks—"

"There's no time for that. Five minutes, he said."

Secco touched Malone's arm. "We'll have to rush him. There's no other way now. We'll use the tear gas first so he won't be able to see Barbara to shoot her—"

Malone twitched and the hand fell away. "You'd gamble on that after what you just saw?"

"I have no choice."

"I have."

"Where are you going?"

Malone walked out into the clear again. The sun had come up and it threw a long extension of him over the grass. He saw it and thought that's me too.

"Furia? You still behind the door?"

The crack widened. "What do you want?"

"Listen. You and Chief Secco both." I've got to stop shaking, why am I shaking, I feel great. "John? I'm going over to the other side."

"What?" Secco cried.

"I'm through. I'm not playing on the team any more."

"What team? What are you talking about?"

"Look at what it's got me."

"Wes," Secco said. "Come back a minute. Let's talk."

"There's nothing to talk about. Not any more."

"But Wes, you can't do a thing like that!"

"Watch me."

"Think of Ellen— "

"Who else am I thinking of? How long do you suppose she'd live with me if I let Bibby die? How long could I live with myself?"

"But this isn't the way to do it—"

Malone took the badge out of his pocket and Secco stopped talking. It said NEW BRADFORD POLICE and the number 7. Lucky seven. He hurled it at the trees. It caught the sun and glittered like a hooked fish. It fell and was lost.

"Furia, you still there?"

"I don't fall for no fuzz trick."

"No trick, Fure. They won't make a deal with you, I will. I know where the payroll money is."

"Where?"

"That's my price. I'll help you get the money back. And get away. You give me back my daughter when you're in the clear. That's the deal. I have no gun and I don't give a damn if you steal a million and live to be a hundred. All I want is my child back and to get her I'm ready to face prison if they arrest me. Deal?"

"And what are your fuzz buddies going to be doing all this time, hold my hand?"

"They'll do what I say. To get you they're going to have to risk shooting me and Barbara, and they won't do that. Will you, John?"

"Won't you think a minute, Wes?" Chief Secco said. "He'll never give you Barbara no matter what you do for him. He'll kill you both after you get him out of New Bradford."

"That's the chance I take."

"If you'll do it my way—"

"I've done it your way. It doesn't work. All I have left is me, myself."

"That's not true."

"It's always been true."

"Than it's always been wrong. Nobody makes it by copping out."

136

"Is that what I'm doing?"

"What would you call it, Wes?"

"All right, then I'm copping out."

"People have to pull together. When we're in the same boat. And we all are."

"Don't preach to me, John."

"Every decent man."

"Every decent man isn't in my spot."

"That's when it's most important! Wes, before it's too late—"

Malone turned his back on the tree. "Furia?"

"Yeah." The spinny voice sounded interested.

"Will you hold off on your five-minute deadline till I can come in and talk to you?"

"What for?"

"You still want that money, don't you? Well, without me you'll never get it. It's in a bank vault."

"In a what?"

"Let me come in and I'll explain the whole thing. You'll never swing the money and a getaway with just Goldie now that you've killed Hinch. You'll need help and I'm your only answer. Do we have a deal?"

"Shut up, Goldie!" The crack widened further. "Okay, you big men out there, I hold off my deadline while your boy tries to sell me. Only I tell you in ABC, if this is some kind of a cop play and you rush the house while we're talking, my first two shots are for Malone and his kid. Put your hands on your head, fuzz, and come on in."

Malone stood loosely in the Thatchers' cold hall while Furia searched him. His eyes were on Barbara. Barbara was sitting on the stairs a few steps up, beside Goldie. Her little fingers were buried in the pile of the stair carpet, clutching. She was staring at her father in disbelief.

"Daddy?"

"Everything's going to be all right, Bibby. You all right?"

"Daddy." She started to get up.

"Keep her there," Furia said, stepping back. "It ain't Old Home Week yet." Goldie pushed her back down without looking away from Malone.

Suffer you bitch.

"It's okay, Bibby, daddy's here, and I'm not leaving you again."

Malone was in a state of excited peace. He had never felt so strong, so secure.

"Never mind with the hearts and flowers, fuzz. Start pitching."

The Colt Trooper was back in Furia's hand, he had reloaded. The Walther was back in his waistband, the rifle was leaning handily against the radiator. The revolver was four feet from Malone's navel.

"We'd better do something about that back door," Malone said. "Just in case. It's broken and eight officers are outside there."

"What do you think I am, some punk? I got a great big freezer and an icebox across it. They start shoving," Furia ripped the Papa Bear mask off and Malone saw his teeth, long and pointed, "bang bang bang. Now what's this crud about a safe deposit box? What kind of a dummy hijacks a heisted payroll and parks it in a bank vault?"

"A smart one," Malone said. "Right, Goldie?"

"Since when did you start bellying up to fuzz?" Goldie wanted to know. "I tell you, Fure, this is a con. I tell you."

"And me with the drop? Relax, doll. I want to hear what's on his fuzz mind. Okay, Malone, it's in a bank vault. How do we get it?"

"Simple," Malone said. "We walk in there and we open the box and we walk out."

"And your buddies let us."

"They'll let us. As long as you have Barbara and me. They'll let us walk out and they won't lift a finger to stop our getaway. Stopping you means Barbara and I die, you've convinced them of that. They won't interfere after I lay it on the line."

Furia looked amused. "And how do we open the box?"

"They'll give us the bank's master key."

The Colt snaked out and bit into Malone's middle.

"You don't have to do that," Malone said. He had not moved. "I'm telling you the truth."

"Yeah? What do you take me for?" His short fuse made Furia's Mickey Mouse ears burn to their points. "You think I don't know how a safe deposit operates? You got to have two keys to open a box, the bank's and yours. So where's the other key? You got it?"

"No."

"Then who?"

"Tell him, Goldie," Malone said.

"Tell him?" Goldie said. "Tell him what? You see what I mean, Fure? He's trying to break us up. That's his con."

"Wait a minute," Furia said. "What's she know about it?"

"She knows all about it," Malone said. "She's the one hijacked that payroll from my house and took it that same day to the Taugus National in town. My wife only saw the pants and jacket and thought it was a man. She's the boxholder, Furia. Look at her. Look at her face."

Goldie's face was like the rest of her, in the deepfreeze. The cold breath had turned her cheeks white with frost.

"He's making it up." Her tongue crept over her lips. "Fure, this is Goldie, remember? Would I lie to you? Did I ever?"

"You say," Furia said to Malone. "How about proving it?"

She had to sign when she rented the box. She signed a phony name, but with the same initials. I got hold of a letter she wrote her sister Nanette, went to the bank, and compared handwritings. They're the same."

"Show me."

"I'll show it to you at the bank. They wouldn't let me have it."

"See?" Goldie said. "See, Fure, he's got nothing. Who you going to believe, him or me?"

"You didn't rent a box at the bank, Goldie?"

"No."

"You ain't got a key?"

"No!"

"I think," Furia said, "we'll have ourselves a look. Come down off there."

"Down where?" Goldie chattered. "What are you going to do to me, Fure?"

"See if you got a key. Go into the room."

Goldie rose. "And if you don't find it on me?" she said shrilly. "You'll let me give this sonofabitch what he's got coming?"

"That's my trip. Get in there. You—kid. Go up in the bedroom."

"What are you going to do?" Goldie said again.

"Bibby," Malone said. "Do what the man says. Go upstairs and stay there till I call you."

Barbara scuttled up to the landing and then she was not there. He had not thought she could move so fast. She still had her baby fat.

"Inside," Furia said to Goldie. He took the rifle with his left hand and brandished it. "You, too, fuzz."

They went into the big living room. A tall fire was blazing away. "Is it all right if I stand near the fire?" Malone asked. "I'm cold."

"You stay put. Them fire tools might give you ideas." Furia squinted at Goldie. "Start stripping."

"What?" Goldie said.

"Take it off."

"In front of him?"

"He's pulling a fast one he won't live long enough to enjoy. Get going, Goldie."

Goldie began to fumble with the zipper at the side of her slacks. "You fuzz bastard, you know how many times I saved your brat from getting her head shot off? This is my thanks!" She kicked her shoes away and stepped out of the slacks. She kicked the slacks in Furia's direction.

"I don't think she'd keep it on her," Malone said. "She's hidden it somewhere."

"Oh, you ain't so sure now," Furia said. "Look in her shoes and slacks."

Malone picked up the shoes. He examined the soles, the linings. He tugged at the heels, tried to twist them. Then he picked up the slacks and went through them. He shook his head.

"The shirt," Furia said to Goldie.

She unbuttoned her blouse and shrugged it off, long gold hair swinging. She flung the blouse at Malone's head. He ran his hands over it with special attention to the seams. He shook his head again.

"Bra," Furia said.

She unhooked it, glaring. It fell to the floor. Malone walked over and picked it up. Her flesh was very near his face and he could see through her sheer pink panties. It left him colder.

He was very thorough searching the bra. The stuffing of the cups would make a good hiding place.

"No," he said.

"Drop your panties," Furia said.

"Fure, how could I hide—?"

"Drop 'em."

She dropped them. She stood there looking at Malone. "I'll kill you," she said. "I'm going to kill you after this, you know that?"

"This part I do personal," Furia said. He stepped behind her. "Bend over, Goldie." She began to curse Malone. The last time he had heard a woman use such

140

language was in an offlimits Greek whorehouse, it had somehow not sounded so bad in broken English. He found himself a little shocked. "Turn around."

"Go to hell, goddam you!"

Furia turned her around gently. After a while he stepped to one side and said, "You struck out, fuzz." He raised the Colt. "I told you not to con me."

"And I told you," Malone said. "She's too smart to hide it on herself."

The revolver hesitated. "Then where?"

"She'd hide it where she could get to it fast. It's got to be somewhere in this house."

Furia glanced over at the sofa. Barbara's coat and hat lay there, and two open suitcases. Evidently he had had the woman pack in the early hours for a quick getaway after he began to suspect Hinch's runout. He waved the revolver. "Her bag. The tan one. Go look."

Malone rummaged through the tan one. He was sure the key was not there and he was right. He went through the other bag for luck. It was not there, either.

When he straightened up Goldie was putting her clothes on and Furia was studying her.

"You know something?" Malone said. "She could have been just smart enough to hide it in Barbara's coat or hat."

"She could," Furia said, "if she ever had it. I'm playing along with you so far, fuzz, but don't take advantage of my good nature. You better start getting results." He gestured with the Colt. "Okay, try your kid's things."

Malone handled Bibby's coat and hat as if they were nothing in particular, as if the warm blue wool and her chubby little body had never met.

"No." He deliberately flung the coat and hat aside. He stood studying Goldie, who was zipping up her slacks. He tried to see into her head. "I know," Malone said. "She hid it on you."

"On me?" Furia said.

"Do you carry a wallet?"

"What the hell do I need a wallet for, Diners Club? You're way out, man." Furia looked angry. "Unless you think I'm dumb. Is that what you think?"

"No, no," Malone said. "It has nothing to do with you, only with her. Why not take a look, Furia? What have you got to lose?"

"Plenty," Furia said. "Rolling over to fuzz for one." But

141

then he said, "Hook your fingers at the back of your neck." Malone hooked his fingers at the back of his neck. "One move and you've had it."

"I'm not going to try anything," Malone said.

"Give me that other gun, Fure," Goldie said. Some spit came out. "Let me be the one."

"Why, Goldie. Ain't you the bloodthirsty one."

"I'll cover him, I mean. While you search yourself."

"You'll do what I tell you." Furia began to paw himself with his left hand. When he was finished with his left side he transferred the Colt to his left hand and felt all over his right side. He even got down in a crouch and ran a finger around the insides of his trouser cuffs. "Okay, Malone, nobody makes a monkey out of me."

"I know," Malone said. "I know now."

"You know what now?"

"I thought she was too smart to hide it on herself. I didn't know how smart she is. She figured nobody would think her stupid enough to do that. Neck. Look at the back of her head. Under her hair."

"Fure, let me kill him!" Goldie screamed.

Furia stood very still.

"Yeah," he said.

He stalked over to her.

She backed off, all the way to the fireplace. She got so close to the fire that Malone was afraid for her hair.

"Fure, I swear to you."

He grabbed her hair and yanked. She yelped and fell against him. He yanked again, downward, and she dropped to her knees.

"I swear, I swear . . ."

Furia took a fistful of the long golden hair at the back of her head and pulled it straight up.

Something was plastered to the back of her skull with adhesive tape.

He ripped it away.

Stuck to the adhesive side, along with some gold and brown hairs, were two flat keys.

"Jesus H. Christ. My own broad." Furia glanced from the safe deposit keys in his left hand to the Colt in his right as if he did not know quite what to do. "You know what I got to do now, Goldie. Don't you?"

Goldie was very fast. "Wait, Fure, wait." Her upturned face schemed with her fear, she was trying to stop him by sheer eye-power. "You kill me and whose going to stay with the kid while you're getting the money back out of the bank? You need me, Fure. You still need me."

"She's right," Malone said. For some reason he was not feeling strong any longer. It was like the tiredness of a week ago, as if none of this had happened.

I'll wake up and Ellen will laugh Loney you're dreaming.

Time came back. "Yeah," Furia said heavily. "What I ought to done, I ought to listened to that yellowbelly Hinch. He always said you were my bag ... Get up, you twotimer bitch. But you ain't my broad no more."

He sounded sad.

"You ain't *nothing*."

Malone stepped out through the front door. The lawn was empty. They had removed Hinch's body.

Behind him Furia spat, "They took the garbage away."

"Don't shoot," Malone called. "It's me." He was wearing the Baby Bear mask. Furia had ordered him to put it on before he delivered his speech. When Malone had balked the little hood said, "It's like you're my boy now, right? Right, Malone?"

"Right," Malone had said.

The sun was well up now. It was going to be a sparkler.

"John?" Malone said. "You can come out from behind the tree. He won't shoot you. No, not the others. Just you."

Chief Secco stepped out from behind his tree.

"You went over," he said. "You really went over."

"There's no time for a sermon, John. I want you to take your men, the whole lot, and clear out of here."

Secco turned away.

"Wait, I'm not through."

Secco turned around.

"We're coming into town—Furia, the woman, Bibby, me—at twelve noon on the dot. There's to be nobody in the bank, John. Nobody, and I mean that. Have Wally Bagshott leave the bank's master key to the boxes on the table outside the vault along with the key to the vault."

"How are you going to open the box without the boxholder's key?" Secco asked almost absently. "You bringing dynamite?"

"I found Goldie's key."

Secco blinked.

"You're to clear the Green, John, the whole area. I don't want anybody or anything on the Green or the side streets, no cars, no trucks, no pedestrians, no shoppers. The stores along Main and along Grange down to Freight Street are to be locked and the salespeople sent home. The offices upstairs in the bank building are to be closed and vacated. You got that?"

"Yes," Secco said.

"Wait, I'm still not through. To make sure there's no interference I want your men and the troopers to line up around the bank, including the parking lot. But without weapons, John. Repeat: unarmed. They're to let us go in, get the money out of the vault, and get out and away. What you choose to do after that is on your own conscience. And John?"

"Yes?"

"You can conceal weapons, you can try throwing tear gas into the bank, there are any number of ways you can stop us. But if that's in your mind I want you to remember: If you don't do just what I said, Barbara and I die first. Furia won't let me carry a weapon, he doesn't trust me. So I'll be helpless. The Vorshek woman will be outside with Barbara waiting and believe me, John, at the first sign of anything wrong she'll kill her, she's worked up a real hate for me because I found the key on her and proved to Furia she was the one stole the payroll from him. They may shoot us anyway after we get clear, like you said. That would be on my head, John. But if you try to queer this, or let the troopers, you'll be as guilty of our deaths as if you pulled the trigger yourself.

"Okay, John, that's it."

Whatever John Secco was thinking—of his responsibilities, of his affections, of victory or defeat as a man and a law officer—the sun on his face did not reflect it.

He raised his arm to the trees.

"You men. We're leaving."

Tuesday

The Payoff

"He's gone off his trolley," Russ Fairhouse said. "There ain't, isn't any precedent for a fool stunt like this, Mrs. Malone. Can't you do something to stop him?"

"What would you suggest?" Ellen said.

They were in the First Selectman's office at a front window diagonally across the Green from the bank. Town hall employees were crowded in other windows peering through the vanes of the venetian blinds. It's like the last scene in that ghastly movie *On The Beach* where there's nothing left on the main street but blowing papers. Ellen had never seen the Green so depopulated, even early Sunday mornings or Saturday nights a half hour after the movies let out. Not a soul but that cordon of state troopers around the bank and they were statues not a muscle moving they didn't look alive. He's got to keep his word, John you've *got* to.

"How would I know?" Selectman Fairhouse said. He was a big man running to lard with beautiful hands, he got a manicure once a week at Dotty's Beauty Salon after hours by special appointment. "All I know is this is not

146

right, Mrs. Malone. It ain't legal or . . . hell, it ain't moral!"

"Neither is a gangster taking a little girl and threatening to kill her."

"But there are other ways—"

"What ways?"

"Then you approve of your husband's action?" Fairhouse asked huffily. "I remind you, Mrs. Malone, he's a paid employee of this town, supposed to be an officer of the law to boot. It makes the whole town look bad!"

"Approve?" Ellen said. "I'll approve of anything that gets my baby back. Thank God for my husband is what I say. And you can take your town and you know what you can do with it."

"He'll go to jail for this!" the selectman said. "If he doesn't get killed by that hood first."

She could almost hear him add *and I hope he does*.

"Would you please let me alone?"

Fairhouse started to say something, changed his mind, stalked back to his desk, sat down, and viciously ripped the end off a cigar. *Who wants this headache anyway. Next election they can wish it on sombody else. A lousy town cop to pull a stunt like this. It will whammy the whole administration. It's all John Secco's fault. The roof falls in about this and over the hill with you my friend.*

Ellen was grateful for his retirement. Her brain was as busy as the Green was empty. *You can't believe your own eyes somctimes, a person finds that out.* Those buildings across the Green looked like falsefronts, the whole thing was taking place on a Hollywood back lot. *All it needs are a camera and a director and there they come to the background music of the noon whistle from the firehouse.*

The black Chrysler sedan went past the town hall at fifteen slow-motion miles an hour.

Ellen got up on her toes and strained.

The blonde woman sat in the rear wearing the Goldilocks mask. *There was just the tip of Barbara's blue hat showing she must have my baby down on the seat oh Bibby mama's here.* The little monster was in the front seat at the right he had a gun to the head of the driver so the driver must be Loney yes it was she could never mistake the set of his shoulders. Loney was wearing the Baby Bear mask and Furia was wearing the Papa Bear mask. *What are they all wearing masks for? It must be that monster's idea of a rib, a thumbnose at the fuzz.*

I don't care.

Just let them be safe afterward.

The Chrysler turned left at the corner.

The Chrysler turned left and rolled to a stop on Grange
just past the corner of Main, headed the wrong way on
the one-way street. Papa Bear got out on the curb side and
waved the Colt Trooper, he held the Walther automatic in
his left hand and the hunting rifle under his left arm. He
was wearing his gloves. The pockets of his Brooks Brothers suit bulged with boxes of ammunition and Malone's
belt with its picket fence of cartridges was strapped about
his waist over the jacket.

A sigh like an afternoon breeze off the river went
through the troopers. Papa Bear glanced at them and
raised the Colt to point into the car. Driver's seat. The
breeze died.

"Okay, Malone."

Baby Bear opened the driver's door and slid dutifully
out from behind the wheel. He came round the hood of
the Chrysler and stopped a yard away from Papa Bear,
glancing into the car and saying something reassuring to the
child. Papa Bear waved the Colt again and Goldilocks got
out on the sidewalk, she pushed the child ahead of her
without letting go, then she shut the car door and backed
against it. Immediately she went into a half squat with her
left arm about the little girl. In this way she was protected
by the body of the car from a rear attack and by the body
of the child from a frontal attack. She gripped Furia's
switchblade with the point just touching the child's throat,
it made the slightest dent in the white flesh. Not for the
perfidious Lady Goldie this time the gun from the royal
arsenal. But the knife would serve nicely as a substitute,
every trooper eye said.

The child was in shock or they had fed her a sedative.
Her lids kept drooping as she tried to keep her father in
focus. The mask he was wearing seemed to confuse her.

Papa Bear looked around. He was in no hurry. His
camera eye swiveled the full 360° of emptiness like a
panoramic shot. It paused briefly one after another at the
empty holsters of the troopers.

When he was through with the inspection he said, "Turn
around." The angle of his masked head jeered at everything.

Baby Bear turned. Papa Bear stepped up to him and touched the muzzle of the revolver to his spine at the third vertebra.

"We go in," Papa Bear decreed. "Hup."

They marched as if a sergeant were chanting cadence up the eight steps of the Taugus National, one behind the other, and went into the bank.

Ellen witnessed the performance through the slats of the town hall window. She saw the Chrysler pull up at the bank the wrong way, she saw Papa Bear get out, she saw her Baby Bear get out, she saw Goldilocks push Barbara onto the walk and grab her and squat with the knife against her throat. Dear Jesus even if she comes away from this alive she'll need a psychiatrist or at least a good psychologist maybe years of therapy oh I don't care just let her stay living.

Ellen saw Papa Bear and Baby Bear make their single-file march into the bank.

That was the beginning of the worst. Because the filming stopped. No, that was wrong, they had already shot the film, it was the projection that stopped, cold dead in the machine. The whole scene was the film including the invisible director and cameraman, they were invisibly part of it along with the visibles. The whole picture froze on the screen outside Fairhouse's window.

Maybe I'm part of it too. And Selectman Fairhouse. And these other people. And the troopers. And the Bears. Maybe we're all part of it, everyone and everything, the Green, the bank, and uneven rooflines of the two-story buildings north south east and west, even the sky and that sun hanging in it like a prop.

It was all frozen on the screen.

Do the images on the frozen screen know about time? Time had simply stopped along with everything else. When she heard the shots and things began moving again she glanced at her wristwatch for the sake of her sanity and saw that thirteen minutes had passed since the two Bears had marched into the bank.

Shots.

Shots?

They had been faint but sharp reports from across the Green, like a sound effect, a drumstick on the rim of a snare drum. Shot shot-shot.

149

Shots *no.*

Why would Furia be shooting oh he wouldn't shoot Loney why should he shoot Loney Loney went over to him. John Secco told me so . . .

"Loney."

As the wail came from her throat Ellen saw the man in the Brooks Brothers suit and the Papa Bear mask burst out of the bank and race down the steps. He had the revolver in his gloved hand and a bulging canvas bag in his left. He ran bent over, almost double.

It was funny how the troopers remained frozen on the film. Couldn't they see him? He was in front of their noses.

Papa Bear flung the canvas bag in the direction of Goldilocks. She threw up an arm in an instinctive grab but it sailed over her head into the rear seat of the Chrysler and she yanked the door open and scrambled in clutching for it.

Papa Bear scooped up the child as if he meant to break her back.

That was when Ellen Malone heard the casting call.

Wesley Malone in the Baby Bear mask with Furia at his heels in the Papa Bear mask marched into the bank. The pressure on Malone's spine increased while Furia looked the situation over. But the bank was a ghost town, he could see that at a glance, no vice-presidents behind the executive desks, no tellers at the windows, no office girls in the rear, everything put away neatly. Like for Sundays.

"Wide open like a broad," Furia said. "They follow orders good. It's a crime." The muzzle prodded. "Don't you want to know what's a crime?"

"Whatever you say," Malone said.

"A wide-open bank. All that bread laying around. Who needs safe deposit boxes with a sweet setup like this?"

"You won't find any money here," Malone said.

"What are you, on the Board of Directors?"

"I know the big squeeze, Bagshott. And Chief Secco. They're not about to let you walk off with the assets. The cash boxes have been emptied and all the cash is in the big vault, the one with the time-lock."

"Stay right there." Furia edged around and got into the tellers' section. He opened one drawer after another. He banged the last one and came back.

"I can dream, can't I?" Furia shrugged. "Not a plugged subway token. I'll have to make out with that twenty-four grand. Okay, fuzz buddy, where's the safe deposit vault?"

Their steps made lonesome sounds across the floor.

On the desk before the vault lay two keys, one to the steel-barred door, the other to the safe deposit boxes.

"You know something?" Furia said. "I'm going to let you open it." He stepped back a few feet, Colt and Walther at waist level.

Malone picked up the vault key and unlocked the steel-barred door. He swung it in and stepped aside.

"Not on your fuzz life," Furia said. "You open the box, pal."

Malone took the bank's master key from the desk and went into the vault.

"You'll need Goldie's key, too," Furia said. He had the key in his left glove. He holstered the automatic and jiggled the key down into his palm. He tossed the key to Malone and leaned against the entrance to the vault. "Box number 535."

Malone began looking for Box 535.

"I'm getting a charge out of this, you know that?" Furia said. "I mean watching a cop pull a bank job. Never thought you'd be doing a no-no like this, huh, Malone? Makes you like one of the bad guys, know what I mean?"

"Here it is." Malone inserted the bank's key into the left keyhole and turned it. Then he used Goldie's key in the righthand keyhole. He pulled. The narrow door swung open. He drew out the flat black box and turned to Furia.

Furia was watching him with what was surely enjoyment. Behind Furia stood John Secco. John Secco's arm was raised. It held a billy club.

The billy club landed over Furia's ear with a water-logged thunk. Everything fell, the Colt Trooper, the hunting rifle, Furia, his hat. The Colt and the rifle struck the floor first. Secco stepped over Furia's body and picked them up. While Malone was getting his mouth in working order Secco plucked the Walther from the holster. He tossed the three weapons to the desk outside the vault and removed Furia's mask. He took a black cloth out of his pocket, held it by opposite corners, and twirled it several times. He stuffed the fat part in Furia's mouth and tied the ends three times at the back of Furia's neck.

Then he straightened up and they stared at each other.

151

"I thought you could use some help, Wes," the chief said. He sounded quite serious, as at morning report.

Malone tore off the Baby Bear mask. He tried to speak and failed. Finally he made it. "You know what you've just done with your help, John? You've cut Barbara's throat. You had no right, you had no goddamned right. I ought to kill you for this."

"Kill me later," Secco said. "We've got Furia in the bag, now the problem is the woman outside, there's a way it can be pulled off or I'd never have started this. You're not a whole lot bigger than Furia, Wes, especially with these built-up heels he wears. Put on his clothes and mask and hat and the gun belt and the rest. The clothes will be a tight fit but with his mask on and if you run crouched over it'll happen so fast the woman won't have time to realize it isn't him." He stooped over the unconscious gunman. "Take your clothes off while I strip him. Don't stand there, Wes. Get cracking."

Malone stood there.

"You going to stand there till she gets suspicious? Undress."

He found himself undressing at the same fast tempo at which Secco was undressing Furia. At first all he could think of was the process. The way you do it first the jacket then the pants then the shirt. Like at night but you keep your shoes on, both pairs are black, maybe she won't notice, I pray she won't notice. That my feet are bigger. Then the other thoughts started in, like why am I doing this and it's all wrong. Or is it. I made my bed and I was lying in it and along comes John Secco and pulls it out from under me. I'll kill him, I meant it, anything goes wrong. But then why do I feel groovy all of a sudden like I'm swinging for the first time in my life. Like we're socking it to 'em.

Hang on Bibby baby!

"We'll take no chances, Wes," Chief Secco was saying rapidly as he helped Malone into Furia's clothes. "He fired three shots into Tom Howland, he fired three quick shots at Sergeant Lombard this morning and another three into Hinch, three quick shots one and two-three seems to be his style, so I'll do it the same, three quick shots one and two-three in here when you're ready. When this Goldie sees you in Furia's getup running out of the bank after the shots like with the money—I've got a canvas bag for you stuffed with newspaper—she's got to think Furia killed you

152

in here, which he damn well might have. So it'll ring true to her. Throw the fake money bag at her, over her head, she's a greedy one, she'll let go of Barbara and make a grab for it. Then all you have to do is snatch Barbara up and we're home free."

"The troopers, they'll think I'm Furia—"

"No, they won't. They won't interfere till you've got Barbara in your arms. Then they'll jump the woman. The troopers have their orders about this, they know my plan, they're carrying concealed weapons. It'll be rough on Ellen, Wes, she's watching from Fairhouse's office, I did my best but I couldn't keep her away, for a few minutes she's going to think you're shot. I'm sorry, but that's the way it's going to have to be. It's got to look right." He yanked Furia's arms around to his back and snapped handcuffs on the slim wrists. "Just so our hood friend doesn't come to and spoil it. Let me look at you."

Malone adjusted the Papa Bear mask.

"You'll make it. All set?"

He nodded and they left the vault. Malone slapped the Walther into his holster and picked up his Colt Trooper, welcome home. Secco went into a drawer of the desk and dug out a fat canvas bag. Malone took it.

"We go," Malone said in his old voice, and he sprinted for the door.

The man in the Brooks Brothers suit and the Papa Bear mask burst out of the bank and raced down the steps. He had the revolver in his gloved right hand and a bulging canvas bank bag in his left. He ran bent over, almost double.

The troopers did not move.

Papa Bear tossed the canvas bag at Goldilocks. She flung up an arm in an instinctive grab but the bag sailed over her head into the rear seat of the Chrysler and she yanked the door open and scrambled in clutching for it.

Malone scooped up his child and the troopers came unglued. Six of them leaped up the steps of the bank and vanished. The rest swarmed over the car. Each man had materialized a hand gun, Malone did not know from where and he did not care. He was too busy making a fuss over Barbara and wondering why she was shrinking from him, he had forgotten that he was wearing the Papa Bear mask. "It's all right, baby, it's me, daddy, don't you remember?" —a stupid thing to say but it was a time for stupidities like that, at least Barbara seemed to think so.

153

At the familiar voice she stopped staring the unbelieving stare he had come to dread and made a pleased sound and slipped her arms around his neck and laid her head on his shoulder as she always did when he carried her up to bed.

Goldie Vorshek was staring at him just as Barbara had, unbelievingly, but as if she could not trust her ears.

She put up no resistance when they took Furia's switch-blade away from her. But when they pulled her out of the Chrysler and reached for the still-closed money bag Goldie hugged it to her breast with both arms like a little girl protecting her dollie and tried to kick and knee every trooper within range. She had two of them writhing on the sidewalk before she was subdued.

Malone watched her capture like the Great Stone Face.

She's the one fed a nine-year-old the booze.

I hope you burn.

That was when the Rams' defensive line hit him.

Ellen tore her child from his grasp as he staggered and transferred Bibby to the other arm and with her small fist dealt him a blow on the chest that landed like a sledge. Before he could yelp uncle she closed in on him again and made a vicious swipe at his mask. The mask ripped and it fell apart.

"Loney?"

She began to cry.

"It's all right for heaven's sake," Malone said peevishly, "I forgot about the mask. Wait till I catch my breath. You hit like Rosey Grier."

"I made you bleed *blood*," Ellen wept, "I've got to cut my nails. Let's go into Sampson's and get it cleaned. Oh, hell, they're closed, aren't they? I left my purse in the town hall like an idiot. Don't you have a hanky? What are you doing in the monster's clothes, you look ridiculous. When I saw you run out like that . . . in his mask . . . How did you *do* it, Loney? It was wonderful. Was it John's idea? I'll bet it was John's idea. Oh, there's John, it *was*. But you were wonderful too, Loney . . ."

"And don't call me Loney!" Malone shouted. "I don't like that goddam name! I never liked it!"

"Why, Loney, I mean—Wes? You never told me."

"I'm telling you now! I hate it."

"Yes, Loney, I mean . . . Bibby darling, it's all right. Mama and daddy aren't fighting."

She mothered her child while he stripped off the fragments of Papa Bear mask and threw them away in disgust.

154

He felt around in Furia's pockets until he located a handkerchief. It looked antiseptically clean. For some reason this riled Malone. He applied the handkerchief to his wound still churned up.

After John Secco came the troopers, out of the bank, bringing Furia. Blood was still coming down Furia's face and he was stumbling along like a robot with gasket missing, they had to half carry him. His underwear was too big for him and his hairy shanks and bandylegs were pimpled with cold. A trooper came running up with something that looked like a horse blanket and threw it around him. Furia clutched it to him, shivering. His bugged eyes passed over Malone, Ellen, Barbara without recognition, it was Goldie Vorshek they were hunting. They located her in the grip of three troopers in the Chrysler and in a flash he became Man-Mountain Furia, hero of his dreams, too-big underwear, skinniness, goose pimples and all, in a last struggle for status. He kicked and bit and butted and threw himself from side to side with troopers hanging on to his arms and legs, spinning out an endless line of dirty words, the spin whirled up to a screech, it was laughable and somehow sad, too. A trooper finally ended his nonsense with a well-placed slap and they pushed a cooled-off bad man into a state police car, threw the blanket in after him, and sped off. Another police car pulled up and they transferred a sullen Goldie Vorshek to it and then they were gone, too, along with Chief Secco, who gave the Malones a neighborly wave.

Leaving Mr. and Mrs. Wesley Malone and daughter on the empty corner of the empty street facing the empty Green. It never looked so empty, not even when the film stopped cold.

But then Wallace L. Bagshott creeps through the entrance to the upper floor of the bank building into the lobby, he's been hiding upstairs in Judge Trudeau's law office. He peers out at the Malones, shakes his head, hurries into his bank, and locks the doors. He's headed straight for the bottle of Canadian Club parked in the bottom drawer of his desk that he thinks nobody knows about.

Jerry Sampson opens the doors of his drug store and sticks his head out timidly. He's been hiding behind his prescription counter. He waves over at the Malone family and then wipes his balding head as though it were an August day.

Arthur McArthur Sanford in his Nehru jacket and oriental carpet slippers reopens the stationery and book store, he keeps a running stock of at least three dozen books on display behind an amber translucency, Arthur is a one-man committee to push culture in New Bradford and not getting very far.

Lew Adams with his Theodore Roosevelt mustache preceding him comes out of nowhere and begins taking down the ironwork in front of his jewelry shop. He keeps looking over his shoulder.

On Grange Street running all the way down to Freight stores are reopening, the proprietors were on the premises all the time.

Beyond the Green First Selectman Russ Fairhouse bursts out of the town hall followed by a crowd, they stream over the grass past the bandstand that hasn't heard a tootle in forty years but it's kept in a nice dress of paint for old times' sake, ditto the World War I tank.

Toward the Malone family.

A herd of cars comes running down Main Street from the north alongside the Green to the accompaniment of bawling horns. Cars shoot up to curbs, people pile out even on the Positively No Parking At Any Time side.

Headed for the Malones.

Racing across the bridge from the other side of the Tonekeneke come Young Tru (Hyatt), Edie Golub, old Ave Elwood, and Marie Griggs (she's Ave's night counter girl but she's been filling in today for a day girl who called in sick).

Seems like the whole town's massing, all sizes and shapes and ages (including the Don James family and New Bradford's nine other families of color, *they're* beginning to move in and some people are getting worried). Including Joe Barron of the Army Navy Store who's been trying to organize a Human Relations group, he's pretty new in town, and Marie's boy friend Jimmy Wyckoff, and fat Dotty from the beauty salon, and Father Weil striding along in his cassock and collar (there's really nothing going on at the Romish church this time of day on a Tuesday but the good Father has a flair for drama, it keeps the Church in the public eye, like that's why clergymen in films are always Roman or at least Episcopalian, the Episcoloopians' high church boys wear turned-around collars too, the Prottier ministers are the forgotten clergy) . . . the whole town has come out for the tar-and-feathering

156

or the bazaar or the auction or whatever it is that's going on. And they're all bearing down on ex-Officer or is it still Officer Wesley Malone and his girls asking questions, how did they find out so fast, you can't keep anything hushed up in New Bradford but this one breaks all the speed records, while Ellen drinks it up like a thirsty grunt after a dry duty and Malone watches her with wonder, to listen to Ellen chattering away you'd never know what she's just been through.

And Malone is feeling a sneaky glow himself. Like when he took a couple too many belts at the wedding and they spent the first three hours of their honeymoon night in the motel bathroom while Ellen held his head over the toilet bowl. Malone is feeling the sneaky glow that you feel like when you have first dug the Sermon on the Mount or some of that Golden Rule stuff the priests and ministers and rabbis are always spouting on the desert air, or learned about no man being an island or however it was the guy said it, or in other words when you have joined the human race.

It is not late enough in the day for old Sol to be going down over the People which would sort of symbolize Wes Malone's sneaky glow, it is still barely past the halfway mark between sunrise and sunset.

So we just count our blessings and fade out.

Other SIGNET Suspense Novels
You Will Want to Read

☐ **COUNTDOWN FOR A SPY by Don Von Elsner.** A carefree vacationer on the exotic island of Hawaii, secret agent David Denning suddenly finds himself playing a key role in forestalling world cataclysm. (#D2829—50¢)

☐ **DEATH TO MY BELOVED by Richard Neely.** A psychotic killer lashes vengeance from San Francisco to New York leaving a scarlet trail of murder, blackmail and sex, and a publisher's empire falls in an explosion of scandal. (#P3742—60¢)

☐ **THE INVISIBLES by James Dark.** With the help of a voluptuous voodoo believer Mark Hood sets out to trap a successful revolutionary who threatens to destroy Miami. (#P3956—60¢)

☐ **ODDS ON by John Lange.** A unique mystery, in which three ingenious gentlemen utilize an IBM computer to mastermind a million dollar heist. (#P3068—60¢)

☐ **GIDEON'S RISK by J. J. Marric.** The incomparable Commander Gideon risks his career to trap the most elusive of criminals, the respectable and influential citizen. "A whirl of tenterhooks, arranged with practcial skill."— New York Herald Tribune (#P3143—60¢)
